Changeling Press, LLC

ChangelingPress.com

Commanded

Ashlynn Monroe

Commanded

Ashlynn Monroe

All rights reserved.
Copyright ©2022 Ashlynn Monroe

ISBN: 978-1-60521-820-5

Publisher:
Changeling Press LLC
315 N. Centre St.
Martinsburg, WV 25404
ChangelingPress.com

Printed in the U.S.A.

Editor: Margaret Riley
Cover Artist: Angela Knight

The individual stories in this anthology have been previously released in E-Book format.

Table of Contents

His to Command (Commanded 1)

Ashlynn Monroe

A nameless orphan growing up as a servant in the king's household, Brisa learned to survive by adapting. Her closeness in age to Princess Val'Trea put her in place as the princess's lady maiden, her most trusted personal servant, but Brisa's look-alike appearance makes her Val'Trea's commanded stand-in.

Ka'Sen, Prince of Planets, Leader of the Union of Worlds, can have anything he wants, except magic. The sacred home world turned from technology during the great exodus and saved the dying planet by finding magic. Those on Rosrel protect the mystical forces from outsiders. Ka'Sen knows such power would quell his enemies and cement his father's legacy. He must convince the Rosrel princess to become his wife and give him a child of magic.

Brisa never dreamed the princess would command her to wed on her behalf. When nothing, not even your face, belongs to you, how do you find the courage to say no?

Prologue

Ten Years Earlier

Pain radiated over the delicate skin covering Brisa's bare back. The whoosh of the cane made her stiffen a moment before the hateful rod cracked against her body. She shook but refused to cry. They stood in the cold stable yard. Wind numbed her, and she was grateful for the small blessing from the Mother even as the stench from the stables carried past her.

"This should be more satisfying," grumbled Marta, the cook. "If she were dressed a little finer, imagining the princess is getting her due would be easier. They look so alike with that wavy brown hair and green eyes."

A mare whinnied in the distance. The sounds of the bustling activity in the inner bailey didn't cover the harsh words.

Someone behind Brisa cleared his throat. "They could be twins, but you're right, it's not the same to beat this one, even if she's probably the king's girl, too." His voice was dry and raspy. "I always knew the old bastard had his way with the sluts in the village." The sound of the man spitting made Brisa cringe. "The old devil might wear his crown everywhere he goes, but he doesn't seem to remember to keep his britches on."

To speak of the king as they did was more stupidity than courage.

The cane found its mark again, distracting her from the conversation, and this time a squeak of agony escaped before Brisa could stop herself. Two young boys ran past, stopped to stare, and then hurried away.

"Hush up, or I'll add an extra lash!" This voice

was Sir Wal'Tar, the oldest guard in the castle. She knew he had no love for her because of her face, something she could not control. She vowed to be kinder to the man, even as the next lash caused tears to well in her eyes. Maybe he would hate her less after he got this bile out of his system.

Actions were the only way to show people she was not Princess Val'Trea.

More pain exploded across her shoulders. The princess's punishment would be over soon. It had to be.

"Shouldn't Princess Val'Trea be here to see the damage her behavior caused?" Madam Anna, the tutor, asked. "I don't understand the purpose of beating another child. Our princess has refused to memorize the charter, but tormenting her lady maiden won't change her attitude if she doesn't know the girl is suffering."

Marta laughed. "Oh, you're a silly chit. This is why tutors never last long. Last time, she saw, and she took the cane and gave Brisa seven more lashes just for fun. Poor thing passed out. She lost a lot of blood. Just pretend it's the princess. These punishments are for us to get our anger out more than for the princess's sake."

"Dear Goddess! Stop! I had no idea." Madam Anna's distress registered through Brisa's pain.

Sir Wal'Tar cleared his throat. "I. Will. Do. My. Duty." Irritation hung on his every syllable.

The final lash landed so hard Brisa's knees gave out, and she landed on the ground. Her legs shook as she tried to stand. Blood saturated her damaged dress as the fabric rubbed against her wounds.

"Nine years old," Madam Anna sighed. "This form of punishment transference is unspeakable. I will talk to the king."

Marta gave a dry laugh as she covered Brisa's bloody back with a shawl. "You'll be thrown out. You seem kind, but do not pretend to know what is best for this castle or kingdom. Brisa is a good girl, many have taken a hand in raising her. If you want to do right by her, keep the princess in check. If you take Val'Trea's behavior to His Majesty, this child will suffer, not the princess." Marta's voice was uncharacteristically kind. Maybe it was the blood loss, but Brisa thought she heard regret. "She was left here as an infant, proof of the king diddling the village girls by the look of her, but she'll never be more than a servant in this house. Do not imagine the king cares. His love is for his daughter, not his bastard."

Brisa flinched. She didn't know if the king was her father, but the idea he might know she was his and still not love her hurt. She must have had a mother and father somewhere, but they hadn't wanted her. She'd been left on the castle's kitchen doorstep as a foundling. She couldn't say she loved the parents she'd never known any more than they'd loved her. Taking a wobbly step forward, she tried to hold her head high. If she let the adults know how much she hurt they'd win some undefinable prize.

Madam Anna hurried over and took her arm. Her blue eyes were red, as if she'd been crying. The others all shuffled off in separate directions. When Brisa looked up at the teacher, she tried not to let her emotion show. She focused on something to keep her mind busy.

"The Charter of Rosrel is a sacred bond between the Royal House of Lyxon and the people of Rosrel," Brisa's voice wavered. "From today, and for all days to come, the first article states that all men who take a wife will not be forced to relinquish that woman or her offspring to the authorities unless this woman commits a crime punishable by au -- author -- authorized rule. Article…"

"You can stop," Madam Anna interrupted. "You're a good student. You've done well by your mistress's side. I'm so sorry. I just want the princess to grow in her knowledge."

"This is the way of things." There was no use being angry at Madam Anna. Brisa sighed. "Others have chosen the battles to fight over her behavior, but I am always the casualty in the war."

"You speak as if you're an adult. It's easy to forget just how young you are. Until today I assumed you had a mother in the castle."

"I have never known a mother, but the Goddess is everyone's mother, isn't she?"

"Yes, I suppose she is."

"And I have enough to eat, serviceable clothing, and a good education. Many village girls have mothers, but none of those things."

"You may look like the princess, but that is where the similarity ends." Madam Anna smiled, but the corners of her mouth wobbled as if holding the expression was causing her distress. "You are a very brave girl."

Brisa held her hands over her eyes to hide the unshed tears. "I am practical. The princess is my greatest friend and worst enemy. I have been raised to see to her happiness. It is an odd life, but without this duty I would spend my time in the kitchen with Marta, peeling carrots until my fingers bleed, or working in the field until my back breaks. Terrible things often happen to orphans. The life I have is a gift. Every gift has a price, so says the Mother. Someday, she will take me from here to live as her Daughter in the sky."

Brisa didn't look at her teacher. She didn't want the woman to know what she'd let herself hope -- believe. When she lay in bed wanting to cry, she remembered her prayers instead. She was the Mother's true Daughter. Saying the liturgies always kept her eyes dry. She repeated them mentally now, for strength.

"I have seen you reading your prayer books. Each morning you come from the chapel before classes. Do you hope to devote your life to the Mother Goddess? I do not believe the king would invest so much money in raising you to be a lady maiden if he wanted you to join the clergy."

"We are all members of the Mother's ministry. I can serve both ladies without having to choose, or so the priestess tells me." Pain returned as the adrenaline wore away, and her vision blurred. In the distance, she swore she saw the outline of a woman standing by the trees. Reaching toward the shadow, she stopped herself from calling out *Mother*...

She stumbled, falling to her knees. Mistress Anna knelt next to her in concern.

Brisa's lower lip trembled. She reached again. *Mother.* She'd always felt watched over, cared for, by something unseen. *Mother.* Fevered dreams of a desperate mind. Still...

Mother? Maybe she hadn't been abandoned by some terrified woman, maybe she was being tested. Prophecy said the Mother had a Daughter among the people in every generation.

"We need to take you to the healer."

"Please, no. I want my doll." Tears sprang to Brisa's eyes. She just wanted to go to her bed to heal. She had her magic. That wasn't some coincidence. None had been named Daughter, yet. Even the king couldn't deny the Mother. If she was pious, maybe it would be her. The Mother Goddess was her mother. If she could just be named, she would have a purpose.

As she gazed into the distance, her vision narrowed to pinpoints, and her strength ebbed. The princess was a picky eater, and Brisa was only allowed to consume the grains and fruit the princess wanted, so she never felt full. She suspected the cakes and candies the other girl snuck kept her from suffering the same fate, but there was nothing Brisa could do besides eating every bite she was allowed. Lately, she'd wondered if Val'Trea was trying to starve her intentionally.

Madam Anna picked Brisa up. She couldn't remember anyone carrying her before. At her age, she should be too heavy. She tried to protest, but she couldn't form the words. Her head rolled back, and she gazed up into her teacher's face. The ashen pallor of her tutor's cheeks made her feel a sense of guilty relief. The woman would be less likely to call down the king's wrath on Val'Trea in the future. She looked out toward the trees, but her vision of the Mother was gone. Her mother had left her in the hands of a stranger again.

Chapter One

Brisa knelt next to the sick girl, Nela, feeling her forehead. Her littles. She'd become a magnet for orphans after she'd started taking food to the village. During the great drought, she'd seen the body of a child dead of starvation. The sight still tormented her in her nightmares.

The long-abandoned temple to the old gods now served the Mother Goddess. There was poetry to repurposing the building, but for good measure, she'd removed every face from the ancient frescos to the sacrilegious deities. This drafty old relic finally made the word home hold meaning because of the people who sheltered here. This was the first place she'd felt loved.

Meglena, the oldest of her littles, was only a few years younger than she was. She pushed her long, curly blonde locks out of her eyes as she went through the basket of food Brisa'd brought to this hodgepodge group. Marta, the cook, knew she took the food, and strangely, never protested. She'd learned the woman had once been an orphan herself. While there was no love between them, she sensed the woman held a grudging respect, and that was enough.

Brisa glanced over at Meglena. "How long has she been like this?"

Meglena took the tiny hand and held it tight. "Three, maybe four days. Why have you been gone so long? It's been over a week."

Brisa bit her lip. She hated to hurt the girl. Meglena had been the closest thing to a real friend Brisa ever had. Her orphans occasionally expressed worry that her interest would wane, but that was ridiculous. Coming here gave her a purpose, and she needed her littles as much as they needed her.

Brisa shivered as she looked at the rows of tiny pallets filled with sick children. *Goddess help me. I can't lose them, any of them.* The happiness on each tiny face when they saw her was addictive. *I will go to the temple and make vows of sacrifice. Please, Goddess. Whatever you want of me, it is yours.*

Brisa shook her head, hating to say the words out loud. "The grand ball. Some tech prince is coming from the beyond, and everything at the castle is in an uproar. I haven't been allowed any escape until now."

"You should have come sooner. They're all so sick." Meglena coughed.

Before the girl could protest Brisa touched her forehead. It was damp and overly warm. "You're ill, too."

"Someone had to care for them. When you're not here, I am who they look to."

Guilt shattered through Brisa. She'd always encouraged the littles to follow Meglena, to trust her. She'd never asked the girl if she wanted the role. "Get into your bed. I'm here now. I will take the lashing. It's not as if another scar or two will make a difference."

Meglena's stricken expression instantly made Brisa regret her glib comment. "I jest."

"Do they beat you when you come here?" Meglena coughed hard, her pale face flushing.

"Get into bed," Brisa ordered. "I am the lady maiden of the princess. Who could be safer?" The lie dripped from her tongue, and Meglena sagged as Brisa led her over to the small cot and tucked her in. "Rest. I will spend the night."

"But the princess…"

"Is having a dress fitting. I doubt she'll miss me." Another lie. She tried not to think about how easily the fib came. *Mother, forgive me.* She'd atone later.

Of the seven orphans who'd taken shelter in the abandoned temple, only Meglena was of marriageable age. The pretty girl could find a husband, but Brisa suspected she didn't want to leave the littles alone. The oldest of the other girls was only nine-years-old. Children came and went, and Brisa did what she could. Often she had been instrumental in finding them a happy, safe place.

Brisa leaned down to pull the tattered blanket more snugly around Hoda, the precocious five-year-old many thought was another one of the king's bastards. She looked so much like Brisa they could be sisters. She grinned when she noticed Hoda clutching the straw doll she'd passed down. That little doll had been her comfort for many years. Seeing the doll help a child who was likely her half-sister sleep through a fever gave her a melancholy joy. Hoda shared the same coloring as both she and Val'Trea, right down to the unnaturally green eyes that others often commented on.

Smoothing the brown curls off the girl's brow, she noticed Hoda's forehead burned hotter. The decaying temple let in too much cold. Winter was coming early. They needed more blankets and firewood. She'd brought a good supply of food, but realized they'd need a strong broth. She set a kettle of water over the fire.

When all the girls, even Meglena, were sleeping, Brisa stood and left as quietly as she could. Twilight's orange sunset was burning off into the gray light before nightfall. The stones were damp under her feet and the cold reached through the thin fabric of her slippers. Some houses were still dark, but most had the warm light of hearth fires lit. The shops were closed as the villagers tucked in for the night. Brisa hurried through the village to find Lee. He was a good man. He would help.

"Hey," called the baker's son. "Safety in the sleeping hours."

Brisa stumbled over to him and gave him a nod. "Safe sleep to you, as well."

He nodded back. "Take this to Meglena, please." He handed her a wrapped loaf.

She tried to hide her grin. They'd be a good match, this chubby, ruddy-faced boy, and her friend. He had a promising future. "I will. Thank you. Have you seen Lee?"

"He's over at the tavern. Cards."

She'd heard of his skill, but she'd never been inside the tavern. "Could you ask him to come see me at the temple?"

The boy laughed. "My father would kill me for going in there. *Den of reprobates* he calls it. Sorry."

She shrugged. "Thank you for your kindness to Meglena. She is my heart sister."

He nodded. "You have done many things I would call kindness concerning our village. My gifting food to a pretty girl is purely selfish." He grinned broadly. "But I'm sure you already know I wish to court her."

She sensed he was asking her permission, even though she had no right to expect it. The gesture made her like him even more. "You can court her, and if she's smart, she'll let you."

His face reddened brighter than its naturally jolly color. Brisa put her hand on his shoulder. "I'll see she knows who to thank for the gift. She's a bit under the weather, but when she feels better, I'm sure she'll come see you."

"Under the weather? What ails her?" His concern was intense and proved his feelings.

"It's fever. Please keep this between us. You know how illness panics. I need Lee to help me get them wood to stay warm."

"They're all sick?" Now he sounded worried for more than just Meglena.

"No," she lied. "It's just that the littles are so small. I was hoping Lee could help with the chore, that's all."

He let go of a breath, and his shoulders sagged. "That's good. I'm sorry I can't go get him for you."

"I'm glad you are obedient to your father. On the morrow."

"On the morrow, Lady Brisa."

She bristled at the honorary title, but hid the reaction with a polite smile before rushing off toward the tavern. Laughter and noise streamed out of the well lit stone building. Women of low reputation walked with men down the path, and she saw a stable boy watering the horses of a newcomer. She paused, nervous about going farther, but her littles needed her to have courage. She wasn't a child anymore for Goddess's sake. Straightening her shoulders, she walked ahead as if this was a normal visit for her.

Lee. Thinking of him made her smile. He'd be surprised to see her in the tavern. Lee. So reliable. Such a good friend. He'd been helping her since the beginning. He'd seen her trying to carry a little boy who was almost as tall as she was. He'd taken him from her arms and helped her get him to the temple where she'd managed to save his frozen legs. That little boy was a farm hand now, but he often brought the temple children fresh food. He knew her favorite was rabbit and always snared one for her when he came. Without Lee, she might not have been able to save him.

As they'd grown older, she'd expected him to marry, but he hadn't. She wasn't sure why, but his marital status mattered to her more than it had the right to. She never doubted he'd be there for her, but if he wed that would need to change.

Nervousness fluttered in her stomach as she stepped up onto the long porch and took hold of the heavy door handle to gain entrance into the drinking establishment. She'd never been inside the busy gathering place. It was not the kind of place princesses or ladies went. Lucky for her littles, she was neither.

Peering through the doorway, she tried not to be noticed, but it was clear this was a male domain. *Lee*. His blond head bobbed. He needed a haircut. She watched his handsome face morph into a huge smile as he threw his hand down on the table. His companions wore angry or miserable expressions. When he glanced up, he gave a double take in her direction before grabbing his mug and draining the contents. Half standing, he scraped the money in the center of the table into a pile before shoving fistfuls into his pockets.

One of the angry looking men grabbed his arm. "Hey! Give me the chance to win it back."

Lee glared at the hand, and the man let go. Lee scowled. "Later." He hurried over to her, guiding her out into the darkness. "That's no place for you. I was starting to worry. Another day and I'd have stormed the castle."

"I'm fine. It's just been very busy."

"I heard. A sky ruler is coming here. Never thought I'd see that. They've been banned for so long I'm surprised the king will allow it."

"My mistress is excited. Considering how badly the tech worlds want magic I suspect the king needs money. Val'Trea has been getting fitted for new dresses and very focused on the attention, but I don't think she understands why the king is lavishing so many resources on her. I believe there will be a match."

Lee's blue eyes narrowed. "Would she force you to leave?"

"Yes. Unless by the grace of the Mother Goddess this sky ruler doesn't allow her to bring me. We don't know their culture. Maybe a lady's maiden isn't important in his land."

"If it comes to it, run with me. I will protect you." His words froze in the chilly air. When he took her face in his hands, his fingers were warm despite the cold. "I refuse to lose you."

Heat burned in her cheeks. "What are you saying?"

"I'm saying run with me. Be mine. The king has a long shadow, but every shadow is chased by the sun. We'll find someplace, far from here, where we can live in the brightness. I want you for my wife. Don't go back to the castle tonight."

Her mouth went dry. She'd never let herself imagine that life, purposefully avoiding the thoughts to protect her heart. Now he was shining a light on her darkest hopes with hateful radiance. Her throat tightened. The scent of winter hung in the air.

The chill reminded her why she couldn't follow him and her traitorous heart. "They're sick."

"Who? The princess?"

"No. Lee, my littles are sick, and Meglena too. Please, I came to ask you for help."

His eyes darkened. "Damn the Goddess!"

"Lee! Don't say such a thing."

He flushed. "Sorry," he mumbled. Then he pulled her close, hugging her tight. The sound of night creatures sang all around them. A chill swirled, but something warm burned between them. His check rested on the top of her head. "I am yours to command." His words muffled against her hair.

"You wouldn't have broken my heart if that were true. Let us forget what can never be and accept what is here today. Please, we need to warm them."

"I wish I could find solace in the moment, but I can see our sunshine in the distance, and all I want to do is drag you away from the long night. I fear for you."

"Right now, we need to fear for the littles. Come."

He followed her down the path. Rocks and dry leaves crunched under their feet as they hurried along.

The fire had died low, and she hurried inside to add to more tinder. The water was hot, but not boiling yet. She threw in some dried meat and the last of the harvest vegetables. A weak broth was better than none.

"What's wrong with them?" Lee's voice was heavy with concern.

"Fever. I'm not sure what type. They don't have the gray."

"Thank Goddess. But fever is dangerous. We can't risk bringing the doctor. Rumors of winter lung or the gray will have the town in an uproar. The village will burn them in their beds."

"I know." Terror made her weak in the knees. "I'll bring medicine from the castle."

"How will you ever sneak that much medicine away? It's too dangerous. My mother has roots and herbs she uses to treat the family when the doctor is gone or just charging too much. I can bring some, but not enough for all."

"I need wood. A lot of firewood. We'll move them closer to the flames. I can bring them more blankets. Do you have any furs?"

"I'll see what I can come up with. I'll get the wood in the morning, but for tonight I think we'll get by. Why haven't you asked me about my winnings? That would buy plenty of our needs."

"Because it isn't my business, nor would I ask you to sacrifice."

He grinned. "That money is for us." He reached out and tucked a strand of hair behind her ear. "The moment I learned of the sky ruler I knew I had to get you away from here. You are leaving with me."

She wanted to allow him to order her from this life, but that was just a fantasy. A selfish fantasy. "I wish life was that simple." He had no idea how often she'd stopped Val'Trea from hurting others.

He had no idea how guilty she felt for just wanting the Goddess's love. She was as selfish as the baker's boy with her desire to do good things for her own sake. She wanted to be the Daughter. She needed a purpose. All her sorrow had to mean something. She couldn't just abandon those in the castle to the spiteful wiles of her mistress.

Worry etched tight lines around Lee's mouth. "It's not as if he's come for me." Her words worked. Some of the tension left his handsome features.

"I can feel the shadow looming over us. Time is short."

"The Mother Goddess protects those who love her."

"I know you believe that, but this fear is something so much more primal -- older than your Goddess."

"She's not mine, she's ours. Please, you must hold dear to her too. I need to know you're protected."

His grin broadened into a handsome smile. "You are the most amazingly stubborn woman."

Brisa scowled. "I have had years to learn that art from you."

He shook his head. "This is what I will not give up. Without you, I can't see tomorrow. I will not let some sky ruler lift you up into the stars -- like he's some ancient god taking a virginal human bride."

"You're so dramatic. Besides, if he took me away, I'd just be his virginal servant, not a bride." Heat roared into her cheeks as she realized what she'd said.

Lee glanced away, and she noticed red tinging his high cheekbones above his reddish-blond beard. "When a man has something he cares about, he's an idiot not to hold it tight."

"I'm the *it*?" She tried for levity, but her words came out so softly they made the tension between them worse. She didn't feel some passionate, intense need for him. He didn't inspire the kind of breathless adoration in her that she read of in the ancient love poets, but she liked him, and he made her feel safe. She'd never depended on anyone until Lee.

"No, this magic between us is the *it*. You are just the vessel which has bewitched me."

Brisa flinched and tried to hide her reaction by stirring the pot. He deserved passion. Maybe, if things changed after the sky ruler's visit, she could learn to give him what he deserved. Distracting herself, she focused on cooking and ensuring the broth would be ready for breakfast.

Hoda coughed.

Brisa went to the sick child, helping the girl sit up. There was a disturbing rattle in Hoda's chest.

Blood frothed on the girl's lips. Brisa pounded her back and held a cloth to her mouth as Hoda expelled the vileness from her lungs. She looked over the child's head to exchange a worried glance with Lee.

Lee's brow creased deeply. "I'll go see what my mother can spare."

She nodded. Lee turned to go but looked back at her. She gave him a firm nod. He was her only hope.

* * *

King Vel'Spei extended his hand. The prince didn't smile, nor did he accept the proffered greeting. Vel'Spei dropped his arm, feeling foolish. "Welcome to Rosrel. We have not allowed a mating between the royal house and an outsider since technology was banished. We are very protective of our magic, as you well know."

The prince smiled tightly; there was a cruelty in his eyes that almost made Vel'Spei regret this alliance. Almost. He'd given his daughter all the beautiful things and privileges she'd ever asked for. She could do this for him.

The prince cleared his throat. "I assume I will be meeting my bride, soon?"

"There will be a ball. She is not aware of our terms. I would ask you to make -- an effort."

The prince's smile twisted until his expression was painfully tight. He looked disgusted. "I want a child, a child that carries magic. Nothing more."

The king paused. He took a moment to formulate his words carefully. "I ask nothing but courtesy. Val'Trea is very excited to meet you. There is very little you would need to say or do to win her heart. A woman's love holds a special kind of magic, and it is said power flows with the beating of her heart. It can't hurt to ensure she is amicable toward you."

The prince's dark brows drew together over his dark eyes. He sighed. "There is wisdom in your request. I will consider it carefully. I accept waiting for this ball to meet your daughter. I am not a kind man, but I will not harm her unless she gives me a reason to do so."

The king forced his countenance to remain impassive. His daughter had never been punished or mishandled in her life. She was a soft, foolish child. The idea of handing her over to this foreigner bothered him, but unrest in the north promised rebellion, and he needed the weapons. He needed them very badly. Vel'Spei nodded. "She will not." A handsome face such as this sky ruler possessed could make his Val'Trea compliant and happy. He hoped.

"Good. Show me to my room. My guards remain with me."

"As you wish." The king bowed more from fear than respect. "You are safe here."

"I am Ka'Sen, Prince of Planets, Leader of the Union of Worlds. I am never safe. That will change. With magic in my bloodline, my sons will rule without fear. We will own the universe." He turned, his cape swirling behind him in the singularly most dramatic display Vel'Spei had ever seen. He glanced back. "And you will have our faithful friendship and the protection only a blood alliance can offer."

The king shivered as he watched the young man stalk away. He never shivered. Giving that man magic was the greatest sacrilege. Technology had burned the world long ago. The combination of science and magic would be the worst thing for every planet in the galaxy. No man should have that kind of power.

* * *

Ka'Sen turned to Reven, his most trusted bodyguard, and lifelong friend. "Have you found any trouble?"

"I'm shocked, but magical security is impressive. There are no traces of tech, not even a single communicator. There are no energy signatures for ships either. If revolutionists are hiding here, they don't have any way to leave the planet or communicate off world. This is the safest place in the universe for you right now. Hell, I think I'll take a vacation."

Ka'Sen paused, frowning at Rev, and extended his hand. Rev handed over his digital. Ka'Sen checked the information. "I can't believe there was no fuel signature, not even any natural echoes from the environment."

Rev chuckled. "Always second-guessing me. There were several different elements, but we didn't find any readings indicating from quantity or proximity the presence of fuel. Seriously, this is my new favorite planet. I think you should move here. I might not get any new scars this week."

Rev's sense of humor was the reason he was still alive, but also why Ka'Sen wanted to kill him every time they spoke. "Don't let your guard down. No matter how quiet we've kept this meeting my enemies might be lurking. If they don't come after me, they may kill the woman. I need this too much. Without the king's blessing, I will not be able to leave this world with a bride. Even if I find a noblewoman with a magical bloodline, I'd still have to bargain for her."

"You've never been one for romance." Rev chuckled. "All you have to do is walk into a room and every lady there is yours for the taking, more or less. I don't know if I should envy you or feel sorry for you."

His friend wasn't lying. His power and name

made him a very desirable partner, but until now he'd never wanted to commit to a permanent relationship. He needed his child to have his name, or he probably still wouldn't. "Save the sorrow for yourself. I expect you to protect my bride and children as diligently as you do me."

Rev grinned. He was the only man whose loyalty Ka'Sen had never questioned. The man was his soul brother and the only person who mattered in his life. Every injury his friend earned on the job cut Ka's heart to the quick. This child would bring an end to those attacks.

Chapter Two

Brisa cried out as she was jerked from her bed. The sound stirred Meglena and the littles. "You're wanted at the castle. The princess is angry," Sir Wal'Tar's horrible son, Sir Marger, grumbled.

"Please, at least let me see they have breakfast." Seeing his expression encouraged a change in tactic. "Join us, Sir. It would be an honor."

"I wouldn't eat village gruel." Scowling, Marger surveyed the room with a sweeping glance. "These lazy children should be out of bed. Worthless!"

She realized he didn't know they were ill, and because she couldn't trust him she didn't explain. "It's still early by village standards. I'm sorry I was too tired to travel back to the castle," she lied.

Marger turned his attention away from the children. She breathed a sigh of relief, but then shuddered. He always looked at her in a way that made her feel both dirty and vulnerable. She hated him for it. He grinned, and his rotting teeth turned her stomach. "There's no time. Our beloved princess is very anxious for you. Our guest arrived early. The ball is tonight."

"Tonight! That's too soon." She wiped sleep from her eyes.

"Hurry up." Marger tugged her out the door. Her bare feet ached with the cold as the stone froze her skin. Numbness set in fast causing her to stumble. "I need my shoes and cloak."

"I will keep you close and warm, lovely." He swept her into his arms. "And will you give me the first dance?"

"No."

He set her back on her feet roughly. "I was going to carry you to keep your feet ready for us, but if you won't honor me, you don't need to dance with anyone."

She'd rather crawl on the floor dragging bloodied stumps than spend another moment in Sir Marger's hairy arms, so she didn't protest his actions. Besides, she hated the wasteful extravagance of balls and stately displays. She usually found a quiet corner to stay in until the whole affair was finished if she wasn't forced to stand in for the princess.

To her surprise, another rider approached. Sir Be'tan held out his hand to her, and when she took it, he pulled her onto the horse. Marger scowled.

"Princess Val'Trea has no patience today. She wanted me to see why you dawdled," said Sir Be'tan.

Marger's chubby face reddened. "Dawdled? The girl wasn't even given time to get her shoes!"

Sir Be'tan, a son of a nobleman, was different from many of the other guards at the castle. He'd been born to his title, unlike Sir Wal'Tar and Sir Marger. He had a softer way with women. "Get her things!"

Marger looked as if he wanted to protest.

"Get her things, or I'll see that our princess is told that you put her lady maiden in danger."

Marger paled and shuffled back to the temple.

"Hurry," the nobleman bellowed. He turned her to face him. "I'm sorry for his rough handling, but the princess is very upset. She has ordered you are to stay by her side until the sky ruler has left."

Fear for her littles settled hard in the pit of her stomach, but she nodded. She needed to get medicine to care for them. When the princess took her long afternoon nap or was otherwise occupied Brisa would try to sneak away to the village and make sure all was well. She glanced back at the temple. Marger came out holding her things. He stomped over, shoved her belongings into her hands, and turned.

"Don't forget to apologize," Sir Be'tan ordered.

Marger made a noise like he was choking on his tongue.

"Or the princess will be very displeased with you. Brisa is a very special servant."

Marger's face twisted. "Forgive me, lady."

She nodded. The last thing she wanted was to incur any additional attention or wrath from the brute. As much as she enjoyed watching him squirm, she sensed she'd be the one to pay the price.

"Forward!" Be'tan kicked his heels into the stallion's sides, and he took off. The chilly air stung her face, and she pulled her cloak tight. In minutes, they were back to the castle. Be'tan helped her down, and a stable boy took the reins before the guard offered her his elbow. She put her hand in the crook of his arm, and he led her inside.

Val'Trea rushed down the corridor. Her dressers followed, and a long, flowing morning gown fluttered around her. "Where have you been?"

"The village."

"Ah, your pet orphans. This week is too important for games. I've had a pallet set up in my room. The guards are under orders to stop you if they see us apart. You are not leaving me again. Come."

Brisa followed, fighting to keep her expression neutral. They walked the familiar twists and turns past portraits of long-dead rulers and sculptures depicting wars and heroes. At Val'Trea's bedroom door she turned to the dressers and servants in the entourage. "Wait for us here." She turned to Brisa. "Only you, come."

Together she and her mistress went down another seldom-used corridor. It was very cold in this part of the castle because there was no reason to keep the fireplaces going as these rooms hadn't been used in years, all but the tower room. Val'Trea pulled the key from her waist pouch, and soon they were traversing the many steps curving up to the ancient observatory. This was where Val'Trea practiced her magic. Brisa sensed something dark in the princess, but she tried not to think about that oily sense of evil that sometimes crept over the room while Val'Trea was studying. She'd surpassed her tutors in the art of magic years ago, and took to her solitary study.

Long days sitting here by her mistress's side taught Brisa many things about conjuring that the typical person would never know. Only nobility were allowed magic, but there were pockets of people here and there in the kingdom who possessed the gift. Brisa was one of them. As did the others, she kept her forbidden skills secret.

Val'Trea was proud of her advanced abilities, and what she learned from her tutors was never enough. This was the room where her mistress was the happiest. Truth be told, Brisa enjoyed coming here too. Magic called to her.

Today they weren't here to read dusty volumes of archaic language. Something tingled in Brisa's skull, and she had the feeling trouble was coming -- and that it was coming for her. Val'Trea closed the heavy iron door after she was sure none of the others had followed them.

"I cannot lose my maidenhead," Val'Trea blurted, without preamble. "I learned several months ago my father wishes me to have a child with a foreigner. They've been working out an agreement to trade me for technology. He thinks a handsome face will seduce my compliance."

"I'm so sorry, princess." Brisa kept her voice low and looked down so that none of her fear would betray her selfish reasons for opposing the match. "Perhaps you can explain your desire not to wed to your father. If it's forced, will the sky ruler remain here with you? You would not be expected to leave your world, would you?"

"I would. But I have a plan. If it is only a child he wants, I will give it to him on the condition I remain here. When the child is of age to leave its mother, he may come and collect it. I will be his happy bride, and live the remainder of my days here in my father's home."

Her calculating, cold words made Brisa shiver. "How will staying save your maidenhood? I agree that is a very good compromise to keep you from a life in an unhealthy metal city full of chemicals and death, but you would still need to birth a child."

Val'Trea smiled, but the expression held no warmth. "You see, he has never met me. Men are not very intelligent. I will explain how this world energizes my magic and my fear of leaving stems from losing my abilities."

So far, Brisa was impressed. She'd never considered the princess more than a spoiled fool. Val'Trea was winning a game none knew they played with her. Somehow the idea left Brisa terrified. "There is truth to that?"

"No, but how will this sky ruler know if you, who have lived with me for years, did not?"

"Fair point. I assume, then, your maidenhead has connection to your power?"

Val'Trea's smile was much more genuine this

time. "It does. I only want one thing, to be the most powerful princess this world has ever seen. I'm close. Watch." She went over to a box that sat by the observation slat in the stone. Wind blew light snow inside, and Val'Trea brushed some off the lid of the box as she picked it up. She came over to where Brisa stood.

"Sit down."

Brisa complied, and Val'Trea sat the box on the table between them. "Look."

Removing the lid, she tilted the container so that Brisa saw a dead bird inside. "Why do you have that?" The hair rose on the back of Brisa's neck. This wasn't good. The energy in the room shifted, and Brisa wanted to flee.

"I'm going to make this songbird live again." Val'Trea put her hand over the opening. A soft pinkish light seemed to radiate from her skin. Brisa shivered as she watched the glow intensify.

When the bird sat up, Brisa screamed.

Val'Trea glared. "Quiet down. It will only last a moment."

The bird flew erratically as if confused, scared, and then it made a pitiful sound and dropped to the floor. Brisa's heart raced, and her breath came out in little pants. "Mother Goddess! Sacrilege!"

"Oh, don't be such a pious little ninny." Val'Trea beamed a beautiful, bright smile. "I'm getting better. It flies now."

A sick feeling settled in Brisa's stomach. "How many times have you brought it back?"

"Who's counting? It's cold enough I will be able to keep this one for some time. During the summer I had to keep catching them. I couldn't very well send one of the guards out to collect one for me."

"Princess, this is wrong. Only the Mother holds power over life and death."

Val'Trea's smile turned vicious. "Let me worry about gods and goddesses."

"I still don't understand." Brisa's brows drew together.

"Of course you don't." Val'Trea's words dripped with patronizing sarcasm. "You are going to stand in for me during the wedding."

Brisa's mouth fell open.

"And the wedding night. You will give the foreigner a child. He won't have access to the magic he's after, and I am left unscathed. He'll never know."

Brisa swallowed. Her mouth opened and closed, but only the tiniest squeak came out. She didn't know what to say. Finally, she let out a long breath. "I -- I can't do that for you. You ask too much. You ask I marry a sky ruler who will steal my child. How can you expect that of me?"

"You live here due to my father's kindness. If you are not with child when he leaves, we will find a substitute babe. All will be well."

"I will leave."

"You will not. Your village orphans, the littles as you call them, they're sick." That malicious smile had returned to Val'Trea's face.

"Yes." There was no use denying it.

"I needed something worth trading. If you want them better, you'll consent. Making someone sick is far easier than bringing this little bird back to life. I can take away the illness, or nature can take its course. No medicine in the world will take this away, only magic. If they die, it will be because of you."

Those ominous words stole her hope. There would be no running off with Lee. There was only her mistress's cruel will. She had a little magic, but she had no idea how to wield it beyond a few tiny spells. She wouldn't risk her littles' lives by trying to cast them well. "What choice do I have?"

"You have a choice. You can lie to yourself that I took your options from you, but you have them. Those girls don't have much of a future, but I know you well enough to assume you won't see it that way. You can't fix the world."

Brisa bit her tongue. Val'Trea had the power to fix it, but she wasn't the type to see that any more than Brisa was the type to let children die. "I can't," Brisa agreed. "But I can help my littles. Before I take vows in your place, I want to see the children well. All of them."

The princess nodded. "So be it."

"What happens if the sky ruler finds out he's been fooled?"

"You die. Maybe I die. My father certainly dies. Be very careful you don't give away the game while he's here."

"This isn't a game."

Val'Trea's smile was remorseless. Her perfect white teeth glinted in the dim room. "Life is the greatest game we play. Every decision moves us on the board. I play to win. You, my sweet, are a pawn to be sacrificed." Something flickered in her eyes. "I won't let him take you away, you know. I would miss you too much."

Brisa didn't know what to say, so she said nothing.

Val'Trea went over to her dead bird, picked it up, and dropped it back in the box. "This stays between us. My father would never take a risk like this, not even for my happiness."

"Of course. Assuming my littles grow well quickly."

"After the ball, they'll be back on their feet. I will negotiate a quick marriage."

Brisa fought the urge to be sarcastic. Instead, she nodded. "As long as I can stay and my littles are well. Oh, and one more thing. You must promise me that you'll never use the children against me again. If you don't swear it, our deal is off."

Val'Trea nodded. "I give you my word."

Her word wasn't much, but Brisa didn't have a lot of options. "Then I agree."

"You may go. Speak of this to no one."

"Clearly."

Val'Trea's smile faded. "Yes. Clearly."

Brisa looked away first, unwilling to push Val'Trea further. Her littles were at risk. "Thank you," she mumbled.

"Good. On the morrow, draw a bath. You are the same size as I am. I have had several new dresses left in your room. I thought the pink would make a lovely marriage dress."

Brisa scurried away before she could say or do something she'd regret. There was nothing about this situation she liked, but despite what her mistress believed she didn't have a choice. She wouldn't see Lee again until it was done. She wasn't in love with him in the way he loved her, but she cared for him, and this would hurt him. Everything about this would hurt him. She shivered. And she knew being forced into a marriage bed by some mysterious foreigner from the sky would hurt her.

Walking down the dark stairwell, she tried not to wonder about the sky ruler she'd be marrying -- mating. After having been given up to strangers as an infant the idea of doing the same to her own child bothered her, but that child would be protected by a prince. Her littles had no one to look out for them, no one except her.

Chapter Three

A knock at the door brought Ka'Sen's attention up from his digital. He'd been reading reports on the army's progress. He was sick of war. Magic would even the score. His line wouldn't have to fight for legitimacy if they had magic. "Enter."

Reven's blue eyes appeared haunted. He ran his hand through his blond hair. The smell of wood fire and fresh air clung to him as he entered. He'd already been out patrolling at this early hour.

Ka'Sen set the device aside. "It's early."

"I know. Forgive me, but I came to speak to you about a message your father sent."

Irritation raised one of Ka'Sen's dark brows. "And?"

"He has agreed to give Vel'Spei one ship, crew, three stun bombs, five hundred hand cannons with fuel, and a staff of armory techs who will be able to keep the weapons in order and teach his army how to make more fuel. He will not give the sacred homeworld anything more destructive than this. If that's enough to secure the woman, he wishes you success in your marriage bed and looks forward to a powerful grandchild."

This was so like his father, promise one thing, then change his mind after it was too late for a face-to-face confrontation. Ka'Sen sighed. "Honestly, the idea of giving the sacred homeworld enough firepower to blow itself to the afterlife doesn't appeal to me either. I just need this child. Once the resistance knows we have magic on our side, they'll back down."

"I just wish we could create magic somehow. Why are they the only ones with the power?" Reven squinted, his face held a perplexed expression stirring Ka'Sen to chuckle.

The most ancient of history was forgotten by even earnest scholars. He sighed. It was something he thought about daily. His father's obsession had become his own. "Technology almost destroyed Rosrel when it was called Earth. The exodus for other planets took away all the scientists. Those left behind turned from technology and the old gods. Once the planet returned to a primordial state, magic reemerged, and now it's the most precious thing in the universe. These primitives have no idea of the struggle for power raging in the wider universe." But he did. His father's forces had taken control of one planet after another until the only place they didn't rule was Rosrel.

But the rebels worked tirelessly to undermine their power. Because of the no-tech laws, the rebels couldn't come to Rosrel, and neither could he until this agreement, so he had a chance his father had never enjoyed. He could be the first man with both technology and magic at his side. The long and wearisome negotiation had brought him here for the only thing his power couldn't take -- a bride of magical ancestry.

"Did you want me to bring the new terms to the king?"

"No. I will. Thank you, but if you could establish a prompt meeting, I'll determine if there's any reason to go through with this foolish party. If he's unwilling to accept the new terms, we have no choice but to leave. I wish her father would just hand her over and be done with it. If the girl believes I am here because I've heard tales of her beauty or wit, she isn't very intelligent."

Reven shrugged. "May I advise you one friend to

another?"

"Of course."

"Make the woman believe those things. Make her think you see her as the most delightful female in the universe, and you will have your child. Even if her father says no, she'll run away to be your wife. You are so straightforward you forget not everyone sees the world with such sharp clarity. Blur the edges for this woman, and she will see what you want to show, and nothing more."

He didn't like blurring lines. Playing with her emotions held no appeal. He liked control, and this emotional espionage repulsed him. "I just want the woman to do her duty."

Reven laughed. "You are the smartest man I know, but when it comes to females, you have a serious knowledge gap, my friend. A serious gap. I don't mean to make light of your dilemma, but this poor girl will at least expect a smile."

Ka'Sen frowned.

"Wrong kind of smile. Oh, this is going to be interesting to watch."

Standing, Ka'Sen ran his hand through his hair. He wore his leather pants and boots, but nothing else. "I'm going to get some air."

"It snowed a little last night. Aren't you at least going to put on a shirt?"

"I need to wake up. It's going to be a long day."

He opened the door to his balcony and went outside, in part to escape further conversation, but mostly because he needed to clear his head. Gazing over the landscape, even bleak as it was with the coming winter, he was stunned by the beauty.

The scenery was so intense he almost missed the cloaked figure rushing from the castle. From his high vantage, he could see her long brown ringlets shimmering in the early daylight as they bounced with each of her footfalls. Her profile was lovely. She was small, so much so he had trouble determining her age. She wiped at her face, as if she were crying, and paused to look around. Intrigued, he ignored his body, which had enough of the cold, and remained to watch the female. She went over to the stable and a small boy came out to meet her. She pulled a basket from her cloak. They spoke a moment, and then he took the handle from her. Ka'Sen could see food stuffs as they made the exchange. She kissed the boy on the head, and he hugged her.

The girl looked too young to be the mother of the child, but maybe she was an older sister. Her clothing was much finer than the boy's. The disparity just made him more curious about the woman.

When the boy was gone, she looked around as if she was afraid. He could see her skin was pale and flawless. Her big green eyes were noticeable, even from this distance. She went into the trees, turning back as if she was checking that she was still alone. Then she knelt. Her dark blue cloak stood out against the white virgin snow. He watched as she held out her hands. Light seemed to radiate from her fingers. Something green wriggled from the ground. A bud opened. The large purple and pink flower came to life. His princess. She had to be.

Thoroughly engrossed now, he wondered if his shaking was just from the cold, or in part from the way watching her made him feel. He hadn't expected her to be interesting. She plucked the bloom, kissed it, and stood, brushing the light snow off her knees. Then she turned and ran to the temple. He realized the flower was an offering to her deity. Seeing her left him with many questions. Suddenly interested in a little spiritual guidance, he decided to go to the temple. Returning inside he grabbed his shirt and jacket. He didn't bother to dress like the Rosrelians. Reven was already gone. Ka'Sen was glad he didn't have to explain where he was going.

* * *

Brisa set the flower down on the altar and lit a candle. "Mother, give me strength for what I must do. Just as you nourish your children and protect us, I must find a way to do the same for my littles. Please, give me a sign."

The soft sound of the door opening and then gently thumping into place silenced Brisa. Normally none came so early for prayers. She didn't have much time without the princess's demands, so she took the hours that Val'Trea slept to live what was important in her life. Those precious hours were when she was the most herself.

She kissed the shrine cloth and knelt. Folding her hands, she began a silent chant.

"I have never prayed to a female deity." The gruff male voice startled her from prayer. "What does your goddess expect from a newcomer?"

Brisa turned. He was massive, taller than even Lee. His body was muscular. Under his strange clothing she could see strength. He wore a strange bit of metal at his hip and to her horror she realized it was a weapon. Too frightened to speak she gaped at the stranger, but her gaze kept darting to his weapon.

He took the contraption from its holster and slowly set it down on the floor next to the altar. "I'm not here to hurt you." Then he scowled. "You do speak the universal tongue?"

She nodded, still afraid to say anything.

It was strange how the angrier he became more handsome he grew. His hair was very dark, as were his eyes. He wore no beard, but he was a fully grown man. His skin was as pale as the snow. He looked like something out of the legends, not a flesh-and-blood man.

"Are you a guard in service to the sky ruler?" She licked her dry lips. "The Goddess is mother to all, even those from the beyond."

His brows drew together, as if he were confused.

Brisa found her courage. She'd asked, and the Mother had given. "I've heard rumors those beyond Rosrel do not know of the Mother Goddess's love. Come. Kneel with me and feel her peace. I take solace here often." She held out her hand.

He looked at the offering and then at her face before finally taking her much smaller hand in his. "You're cold," he observed.

"The Mother warms my soul. My hands mean nothing. Close your eyes. Let her flow through you. Just be, and she will find you." Brisa followed her own directions. She felt the male looking at her, but she pushed thoughts of the handsome stranger away as she embraced the pull she always experienced when meditating in the temple. She didn't let go of the man's hand. He shifted. She didn't feel his eyes on her anymore.

It had been a long time since she'd worshipped with someone, and bringing this foreigner into the Mother's presence was deeply nourishing to her faith.

The door opened. "My Lord? The king is ready to speak with you."

Brisa froze. This was not some nameless guard. Her eyes fluttered open, and she turned. He gave her a sad smile. "Thank you for introducing me to your Goddess. I look forward to seeing you later tonight, princess." He pulled her hand to his lips and brushed a kiss against her knuckles before letting her hand go.

When the men left a shaft of light came through the pink glass mosaic window above the altar. The light bathed her offering in a soft glow. "Mother, thank you for the sign. I just wish I understood."

* * *

"He thought you were a princess?" Val'Trea laughed. "I can still salvage our plan, but I need all of you." She turned to Brisa and the dressers. "Prepare Brisa as you would me for tonight."

"But Your Highness…"

"No buts!" Val'Trea interrupted the terrified woman. Given the princess's history of changing her mind, Brisa could sympathize with the servants. This was a dangerous game. "Now!" Val'Trea ordered, and they scrambled to comply.

The women began stripping Brisa.

Val'Trea picked out a pair of shoes and tossed them at the dresser's feet. "She is to look as much like me as possible. Start with an exfoliating scrub down and waxing." The princess went over to her writing desk and pulled out some of her special stationery. "Oh, and put her in a bridal belt."

Brisa's vision narrowed, and she'd have fainted if the woman next to her hadn't shaken her. She wasn't ready for this. "But, we don't know there will be a marriage, not for sure."

"Yes, we do. Fear not, I find you too -- comfortable to lose. I'm going to send a note to the prince explaining my demands. Tonight you get to be a princess." She glared at the servants. "If any of you ever breathe a word of this I'll have your children killed. Nothing you hear leaves this room or they will go to sleep and never wake. Do you understand me?"

The women paled, nodded, and got back to work making Brisa look like a princess.

"What about your father? He'll surely know the difference."

"Remember when we were young? How often you attended the state dinners for me? Did he ever notice?"

"Once."

Val'Trea paused. She straightened from where she bent writing at the desk. "Oh?"

"I thanked him for a gift. He turned and looked at me for a moment. When the dinner was over, he had Sir Wal'Tar take me to the garden and beat me."

Val'Trea laughed. "Remember to think like me. You won't get caught if you act appropriately."

Brisa shuddered. She didn't want to imagine how such a self-centered mind worked. "What are you writing?"

"You will need to know, in case he wants to discuss it. Since you've ruined the original plan, I just have to hope you can pull this part off. I've told him that if he's here to seek a match, I'm agreeable, but I won't leave the planet. We'll marry tonight, I'll give him a child, and when it's old enough, he can return for it. Simple. I wrote a second note to my father telling him something similar. Nelda, take these to the guard outside and ask that they each be delivered immediately."

The girl scurried over to grab the sealed notes and rushed out the door, probably relieved to be away from the dangerous plotting. Brisa wished she could run away too. Instead, she stood diligently as she was physically prepared for something she would never be emotionally prepared to endure.

* * *

Ka'Sen tossed the note down on the bed. He picked up a vase and hurled it at the wall. The glass exploded. His guard rushed in, weapons drawn, and he waved them away. They backed out of the room.

Reven picked up the correspondence and laughed. "You made some impression on the girl."

"I didn't expect her to be a willing bride, but this is insulting." Ka'Sen should be happy. She offered him everything he wanted, but he was angry. The sweet, pious girl in the temple didn't seem calculating enough to make such an extreme offer.

"How is she sure a single coupling will do the job?" Reven laughed until tears leaked out of the corner of his eyes. "I wish I'd seen your encounter."

If the man weren't his oldest and only friend Ka'Sen would have separated his head from his shoulders. "So, what do I wear to my first ball?"

"Don't you mean your first marriage? She could have at least bought you dinner before popping the question like that."

"Shut up. Seriously, Rev. Enough."

Maybe it was the expression on his face, but Reven closed his mouth as the smile on his lips died. "Talk to the girl. You're dancing with her tonight. Find out what's really going on here. I suspect, if she's as deeply rooted in her religion as you said, her resistance could be due to her faith. Maybe you can convince her into a more traditional arrangement if you bring some holy person with you to the ship."

"That's the last damn thing we need."

"Agreed, but if it keeps your new wife content

and pushing out magical babies, isn't that a good compromise?"

Rev wasn't wrong. If this were any other world, he'd just find her, throw her over his shoulder, and take her. But this world was protected by magic, and they weren't going anywhere without the king's assistance. "Now, what do I wear?"

Rev grinned. "I'm going to go ask around and see if we can't get you something she'd expect to see on a Rosrel groom. If you don't look like a scary stranger from the sky, maybe she'll like you better."

Ka'Sen made an obscene gesture, and Rev laughed all the way out of his room. "Is that any way to treat your best man, if they do that here at least? I have a lot of details to find out about. I always thought I'd be hiring Andori strippers for the eve before your wedding."

Ka'Sen threw a boot. Rev ducked, but chuckled all the way out of the room. Ka'Sen watched his friend leave before picking up the digital again. There was so little information about Rosrel to trust. Most of the information was rumor and conjecture. He went back over the military updates, but his mind strayed from their situation to earnest green eyes.

Chapter Four

Brisa stood at the top of the staircase. Val'Trea remained in her room, hiding to avoid any identification issues. Brisa had pretended to be the princess often before that fateful beating. The last time she'd taken on this role the stakes weren't as high. This went far beyond a simple appearance at a boring state dinner.

She walked down the steps, trying not to look at the crowd watching her. His eyes were on her. She didn't have to see the prince to know he was there. Her breath caught in her throat when she caught a glimpse of the tallest man in the room. He wore beautiful ceremonial robes, and his presence owned the room in a way even the king did not. Guards flanked her with casual precision as she walked across the room to the table of food. She picked up a glass of spirits and then set it back down, needing a clear head, before taking a plate and picking out a few small delicacies. She didn't want to eat them as much as she needed something to keep her hands busy.

Lee. What was he doing right now? Worry kept nibbling at her mind. Hopefully, he'd kept the illness quiet. She hated being here instead of with the people she cared about. Most women her age would be in heaven, but she wasn't most women.

Glittering gems hanging in strands from the ceiling of the ballroom caught the candlelight. Prisms danced across the walls. The room was pale shades of gold and cream. She couldn't have cared less. Music floated around her with soft perfection that spoke highly of the musician's talent.

She took a bite of cheese baked in bread, mostly

for show, and the delicate texture was no more than ash in her mouth. If only she could be sure the children had received the food she'd sent with Jaklem. He was one of the children she'd helped to secure a place in the castle. From all accounts, his work in the stable was diligent. He had a natural way with the animals too. He'd been a good fit. She was glad she'd pushed for his position. The boy looked to her as he would family, and she was glad to have one of her orphans close. She gazed off, lost in worry.

"I agree to your terms." His voice sent a shiver down her spine. She didn't need to turn to know the prince spoke behind her. *Her* terms. She could laugh. Val'Trea's terms were brutal. If only she could agree as easily.

She'd do what needed doing. "Thank you," she said softly, her voice strangled around the lump in her throat.

"Your father has spoken to me. All is prepared. Dance with me."

She didn't know what he meant by "All is prepared," but she turned. He was so handsome, but looked strange in the traditional robes of a noble. He was too masculine, and the black formfitting clothing from their meeting in the temple had enhanced everything about him. This outfit wore him and appeared as much of a costume as the clothing she wore. Val'Trea's dress suffocated her very soul. Each step in the princess's shoes pinched with the reminder that she wasn't meant to fit into someone else's life.

When he held out his hand, she set down her plate, moving into his embrace with strange ease. She'd danced with men both young and old, but never with a man who made her heart beat faster. He affected her in ways she didn't understand. They twirled into line and matched pace and synchronicity as if they'd danced together a thousand times. It was disconcerting.

After a series of step, step, twirl the tension of silence became too much to bear. "You dance very well. I haven't given much thought to how others, those in the beyond, live. Is dancing the same everywhere?"

He chuckled darkly. "Is that why you have so consciously lay down on the marriage altar as a human sacrifice? You're afraid to leave what you know?"

Anger coiled in her. He was not a man to mince words, but she was not a woman to be insulted. "You make assumptions about something you know nothing about. I was trying to make polite conversation. Do you handle all your political deals with such brutish negotiation?"

"I thought I was dancing with the most beautiful woman in the room, not negotiating."

He was quick. She paused. The game could be lost far too easily this way. "Then let us dance." She knew he lied about her being the most beautiful woman in the room, but she wouldn't give him the satisfaction of arguing the point.

His arms tightened around her, and they were off. Everything fell away until they were dancing with absolute joy. A new song picked up without a pause, and she realized the performers were accommodating them as the pace of this was faster. Passionate. And they spun. She danced as if stopping would be the end of her universe. And maybe it would be. She wasn't ready for the innocence to turn into something much more intense. She wasn't ready for a man to take her beyond the simplicity of maidenhood.

Panting, she realized everyone in the room was

staring at them, including the king. She could only imagine the beating she'd get this time. Her plan to be as inconspicuous as possible, for a princess, wasn't working. As if sensing her discomfort, the prince maneuvered her off the dance floor and near the drink servers. She reached for watered down wine, and he went for something stronger. "Are you still afraid of me?"

And the game continued. "No," she lied.

He grinned. "I am pleased. For a woman who was so bold on paper, you are less demanding in person."

"Sometimes it is easier to write what must be written."

He scowled. Her words destroyed the playful mood between them, and he drank deeply, but his gaze never broke from hers. Discomfort settled as his gaze weighed her down. She took a step back, unconsciously, but he moved toward her. "I swore I would never take an unwilling woman. Don't make me break that oath."

Her mouth went dry. His words sounded like a threat. Anger rolled through her. "Then don't. I am much smaller than you. If you take me, and I am unwilling, threatening me won't change that. Give me a reason to be willing. Why me?"

He set down his empty glass and grasped her elbow, a little too roughly, as he led her outside into the garden. It was freezing, but after the dancing and heated verbal sparring, she needed the cool air.

"I didn't think this conversation needed curious listeners. If I can control magic, that gives me a weapon I am unable to build. A child with magic holds my legacy, but a wife with magic would certainly help me save lives faster. Why do you refuse to leave with me?"

"I have people here I care about. I have responsibilities."

"Helping your father hold his throne isn't responsibility enough? I offer him a significant protection that will ensure lasting peace here."

They stood in silence for a moment, neither willing to concede the argument to the other. "I'm cold," she whispered. "I'm ready to go back inside."

As she turned he reached out and pulled her into his arms. She gasped, and he pressed his lips to hers. Shock kept her in place, but then a fire, unlike anything she'd ever felt, ignited inside of her. She kissed him back, hard. Her arms wound around his neck. He pressed her close. Even through the bulky robes, she could feel his strength.

This kiss was nothing like she'd expected. His lips made her forget about Lee and her littles. When he let her go, she stood gazing up into his dark eyes, stunned.

"I feel it too."

"What?" Her passion-addled mind didn't understand.

"Lust. This union will be much more pleasant than I'd expected."

She wanted to hit him. She'd never wanted to hit anyone. "I'm happy for you."

His serious expression darkened. "Why must you be so difficult?"

"I. Am. Cold." She fled.

* * *

Ka'Sen watched her go. She'd never said his name. They'd never been properly introduced. She fired his blood like a cannon blast from his destroyer. She was all war and battle ready, but when his lips touched hers, peace he'd never imagined bloomed in him, and he wanted to taste them again. Like an untried boy, he rushed after her, letting her lead him with the unspoken promise of what could be between them.

"Princess Val'Trea," Ka'Sen shouted. Many turned to look, including his stubborn wife-to-be. "Dance with me." She paused, and he pressed his advantage. "Please."

She said nothing as he took her in his arms again. This time when they danced he focused on her face and nothing more. Every change in her expression was language, and he learned. He wanted to savor every moment. If she wouldn't leave with him he wanted to remember tonight, but more than that he wanted to understand his opponent in this battle of desire. He would eventually stand the victor. The prize, her heart, was a treasure he hadn't planned to take, but now that he'd glimpsed it he wanted all of it for himself.

They danced. Time lost meaning. Suddenly, she seemed to notice something and pushed away from him. She glanced between him and the watchers gathered around them and then took off into the crowd. They parted to let her through, and she rushed off like a madwoman. He'd never experienced this feeling of rejection before.

Ka'Sen fought the urge to smash a row of wine decanters on a nearby table as he hurried to follow his runaway princess. He caught a glimpse of her pink dress going through what appeared to be a kitchen door. Curiosity pushed him forward. He walked past a group of servants. "Where is she?"

They all looked like they would faint. When he made eye contact with a little blonde girl, she burst into tears. "For the sake of the gods I didn't come here to eat you, child. Where did the princess go?" The little girl's arm rose, and she pointed to a door. He stalked off and was surprised when the door led outside. He saw something move at the tree line. The shimmer in the darkness had to be her dress.

Resisting the urge to call out to her, he walked through the dying grass. During the day the light snow had melted, but the grass was brown with the promise of winter. He crunched through fallen leaves and pushed the brambles back to enter where he'd seen her go. In a small clearing, he saw her, and suddenly understood her reluctance to leave.

She spoke to a man with blondish-red hair. He wore the clothing of a villager, certainly not a royal or even a noble. They stood close together and when they spoke there was a familiarity between them that enraged Ka'Sen. This man was talking to the woman he considered his. The rough male didn't seem like the kind of man a princess would associate with, but when she wrapped her arms around his waist. When the man hugged her back, tight, possessive, Ka'Sen saw red. He'd never been good at sharing. This princess was his.

"Val'Trea!" Ka'Sen roared. "Come!" Her eyes opened wide, and the village boy rushed away like a coward. He took her hand, without gentleness, and pulled her through the woods. Branches snarled at her hair and dress, but he didn't care. He was done playing. It was time to get married. "I see now why you're resistant to leave. Does your father know about your village lover?"

"He's not my lover. He's a friend."

"Ha. He certainly did seem friendly with you."

Her respirations were harsh as she struggled for a breath. "Where are we going?"

"To get married."

She tried to pull away, but he held tight. "I agree to your terms, but not to you having a lover."

"He's my -- brother. Father has had his share of trysts in the village."

Ka'Sen stopped and pulled her around to face him. Her breath froze in the air. He took off his ridiculous cloak and settled it around her shoulders. "In truth?"

"I am innocent of the relations between a man and woman." Her conviction rang earnestly, and she never broke eye contact.

Some of his anger died. What she said was plausible. The male bore her no resemblance, but he could take after the mother. Ka'Sen didn't trust easily, but he'd seen her with the little boy this morning, another brother perhaps. She might have a plethora of siblings she felt responsible for, and wanted to stay for them. Those motives seemed to fit the sweet girl from the chapel more than a devious female with a secret lover, or the calculating correspondence she'd sent. He didn't like secrets, or lies. Something didn't fit. "We will soon see."

She gasped, but he didn't care that he'd shocked her. This was not the way he'd expected to bring a bride to the altar, tugging her along. The act made him angrier. He pulled her through the castle, and none tried to stop him. They wouldn't have been able to if they'd tried. Her father's eyes widened when they arrived. Surprised when Ka'Sen pulled the breathless princess before the dais where the royal entourage sat enjoying the festivities. "Did you have a child with a village woman?" Ka'Sen demanded, without preamble.

When the king recovered from his shock, he

glared at the princess. She shrank back. Ka'Sen didn't like seeing her fear. He was used to causing fear in others, but seeing this girl's reaction to the old man twisted him up with unexpected ferocity.

Vel'Spei took a moment, let out a long breath, and nodded. "Yes."

Strangeness gravitated between the king and his daughter. Something intense settled in the room's atmosphere. All at the table were silent. Ka'Sen was good at reading situations, but this unspoken moment carried a weight he couldn't decipher as the king's eyes grew sad and Val'Trea's eyes widened.

Ka'Sen didn't understand why the confirmation that she didn't have a lover gave him such a rush of buoyancy. In that moment, he knew he would wed her, and she would belong to no one but him. "We are ready. Let's get this over with."

She made a subtle sound and stiffened beside him. This was no time to placate her feminine wiles. The power of standing beside him, as his wife, would sooth her need for pretty words or whatever it was women believed mattered in courtship. He was certain. He'd taken any female he wanted. This was the first time one had the chance to say no, and to his surprise that made him nervous.

Vel'Spei sputtered, and half stood as he began giving orders. There was a rabble from the guests, and the music abruptly ceased. She appeared dazed. Her expression worried him, but it was too late for her to back out. He wanted her -- a child, he corrected himself. He wanted a child.

A priestess came forward, and his bride tumbled to her knees before the woman. For a second the priestess appeared confused. The holy woman glanced around the room, almost desperate. Her shoulders sagged. This was very odd, but he had no frame of reference for their culture. This spiritual leader dropped to the floor as tears rested on her weathered cheeks, kissing the princess's forehead, and muttering in the obscure language of the land. When the princess looked up into the aged eyes gazing at her, Val'Trea nodded, and the officiant stood.

He was getting sick of this land and its intrigues. He wanted a wife who would do her duty. Nothing more. Or so he kept reminding himself.

The holy woman helped the younger woman to her feet and raised her arms high. Bangles jangled as they slid down her arms. She glanced at his bride before shouting out a call in Universal. "Marriage! Union!" She pierced Ka'Sen with a gaze. "She must accept you." Then she glanced back at the shaking noble woman. "Do you take this man as yours? Will you give him your body, your soul, your future?"

Val'Trea's long brown hair shone in the candle light as she nodded. Ringlets fell forward obscuring her delicate face. "Yes."

"All here are witness. In the oldest way of the Mother Goddess, this woman wishes to join her household with this man. He will care for and protect her. She is his gift, and he will cherish her and the offspring she delivers to him."

He didn't know what that meant. The priestess turned to him. "If she returns to me with one or more of these witnesses to ask that this union be ended, it will dissolve. Go in peace and worship her as the embodiment of the Mother Goddess." She shot the king a subtle glance. "Men who remember those words find happiness that others only long for."

Ka'Sen wasn't in the mood for a lecture. "It's done?"

A sculpted brow rose as the priestess nodded.

"Good." Ka'Sen turned to his new wife. He pulled a pouch from his pocket and took out the heavy bridal necklace. He fastened the thick silver chain around her delicate throat. The intricate silver work rested on the pronounced bones under her neck. She needed a good meal or two if she would carry his strong, magical sons.

She brought her hand to her throat. He ignored the trapped look in her eyes as he scooped her into his arms, and turned toward the staircase.

A rabble of whispers followed him, but he didn't care. The surprised innocence on his woman's face kept his attention. A flutter of nerves made his step falter. He covered quickly, but the reality that he was going to be this woman's first lover made his mouth go dry. He'd conquered worlds, yet this woman ruled him. He wanted to do just as her holiness had commanded and worship at the altar of the junction between this female's thighs until they both saw the gods.

"What -- what are you doing?" Val'Trea whispered.

"I'm consummating our marriage. You promised me a baby."

Her small oval face flushed as her green eyes widened. He'd never seen a woman with such long lashes. She was a beauty. His cock hardened.

When they arrived upstairs, he nodded to his guard. The man rushed to open the door to his room.

"No one is to enter." Ka'Sen looked down at his bride. "Or leave." She paled, but he vowed to ensure she wouldn't want to leave. He'd made love to women all across the galaxy, but sex had never mattered as much as it did now. The door shut securely behind them. "I'll make this good for you."

Her brows drew together. He realized she didn't understand his meaning.

"Prince Ka'Sen --"

"Just Ka'Sen, or Ka'. We're married now. And do I use your title?"

A small smile curved the corners of her lips and, the fear left her expression. "Call me Brisa -- just when we're together."

"Brisa?"

"It's a nickname. Please."

"Brisa." He tested the sound. The feminine moniker fit her so much better than Val'Trea. The name was simple. She was a complicated woman, even in simplicity. He brushed her lips with his, still holding her. Strange, but he didn't want to put her down.

"Ka'Sen." His name sounded like a sigh as she whispered it against his lips.

He pulled back to watch her expression. "I want you. I want you today, and for every tomorrow. Come home with me."

Brisa bit her lip. "I can't."

He scowled, then smirked. "I don't normally ask for what I want."

She brushed hair out of his eyes. "I can tell."

"This is not the last we speak of this." He claimed her lips again. Desire flamed to life between them. He set her on her feet, but their lips didn't separate.

He reached for the tie at her waist. The pink dress opened, and he pushed it off her shoulders. The silk fell away, leaving only the bridal belt made of three thick silk ribbons that covered her most intimate place. When he tried to pull it, she put her hand on his to stop him.

Brisa broke the kiss. "Not like that."

"How?" Confusion made him uncertain for the first time in a very long time. This woman held a power over him that made him uncomfortable.

Her brows drew together. "Don't they have bridal belts in the beyond?"

"No."

She looked at him through her lashes. "You pull the blue first, for harmony. The red is next, for passion. Finally, the purple ensures fertility."

He pulled them, in the order she'd given him, and the ceremonial covering fell away, leaving her naked except for the silver bridal necklace she wore, proof she belonged to him.

"You're overdressed, husband," Brisa whispered. Her cheeks grew delightfully pink.

Ka'Sen shrugged out of his thick robe. His abs tightened as Brisa ran her fingers over his waistband. He made a slight grunting sound but didn't move as Brisa worked the leather down over his hips. Ka'Sen let out a long, slow breath, and she ran her hands down his lower back, then the hard muscles of his ass, and as she pushed his pants off, her fingers skimmed the backs of his thighs. He widened his stance, and his erection bobbed. He'd never been so aroused in his life. She went to her knees before him, her hair cascading in a fall of curls around her.

She was soft and beautiful in a way he hadn't been prepared for. He'd imagined this as a quick act of purpose, but suddenly, every moment had meaning. She ran her fingers gently across his cock, and he shuddered. Anger interrupted his pleasure. "You are a bold surprise."

Brisa glanced up. Her eyes widened. "I did not lie to you."

He scowled. "You are not a virgin."

"Deflowered many of us? I think we are done." He saw hurt and outrage in her expression.

She stood, ready to leave, but he stopped her. "Continue," he ordered as he pushed her to her knees. She seemed prepared to defy him, but obeyed. The sight of her resistance as she gazed up at him, on her knees, his, caused him a moment of such intense desire he almost came just watching the beauty of her submission. In all the universe, he'd never met a woman who'd brought him to the brink so quickly and with such little effort. His breath caught when they made eye contact.

The gods -- goddess -- whatever had given him an amazing gift. Now all he had to do was figure out a way to keep her. As he watched her, he pushed away any thought of questioning her virginity again. He wanted her so much he ached.

She appeared to enjoy the curves and planes of his body as she ran her hands over him. He wanted her to touch his cock, but she didn't. She traced the masculine "V" at his hips and brushed his skin gently, but always her touch moved away seconds before she caressed his cock.

Brisa kissed him where the hair trailed just under his belly button, and he groaned. She blew a gentle stream of air along his shaft and leaned forward to follow the air with her tongue. She lapped at him slowly until he shivered. When she glanced up, their gazes locked again. Electricity sizzled between them. She drew him deeper into her mouth. Her eyes closed, and her small mouth explored every ridge and vein. Her blissful expression only made him hotter, and he couldn't stop watching her.

His ass clenched, and his knees jerked with the

effort to remain standing as pleasure coursed through him. He held the base of her skull gently as he closed his eyes to relish what she did to him.

"Princess, my sweet princess," he breathed. The endearment fit, and he knew from that moment on he'd do everything he could to become her kingdom. She was coming with him. She wanted freedom, but he wanted her.

She lavished his length with attention, but when she turned those long slow licks on his sac, his knees did buckle. He had to hold the wall for support. She ran her nails gently over his lower back and ass. He shivered and cried out. His balls were painfully tight.

Ka'Sen was so close, but he refused to let her rob him of the joy he'd find coming inside her -- with her. He pulled her to her feet. Her eyes widened for a second before he crushed his lips to hers. He wasn't tender as he held her in his arms. The most intense, possessive need he'd ever experienced roared to life. She was limp in his arms for a second before her arms tightened around his neck. When she kissed him back, he groaned and held her tighter.

He slid his hands under her ass and picked her up. She wrapped her legs around his hips, and he could feel her wetness against his shaft. He'd never been with a woman who was so responsive. Her sexuality pleased him. The fact that his body had made her so ready wasn't lost on him. She was amazing. He'd erase the memory of any other man's touch. The kiss never broke as he moved to the bed, still holding her tight.

Chapter Five

Brisa was in control until Ka'Sen lifted her off the floor. His lust nourished her soul and made her complete in a way she couldn't fully understand. His muscles flexed, tensing, as he carried her to bed. She gazed up at him as the kiss broke, and he hovered over her. He touched her face, and his gaze seemed to be searching her expression. "You are mine. Say the words."

She should have been horrified. Instead of terror, he inspired primal want. She wanted him to make the same vow, but she bit her lip and stayed quiet. Ka'Sen eased her thighs apart, opening her to him. He looked up at her. "Tell me!"

"I'm yours," she wailed.

He lavished attention on her clit. She jerked at his touch, shocked. It was easy to be bold when she was caressing him, but no one had touched her like this before.

Ka'Sen lapped at her pussy as if he'd never tasted anything so sweet. At first, she was quiet, and then her whimpers grew. He lapped faster, harder. She tangled her fingers in his hair, bucking against his face. Brisa cried out, and he didn't stop. She was breathing harder, and her whimpers grew more desperate. She squeezed her eyes shut and saw sparks behind her eyelids as her passion teetered toward the precipice of something wonderful. She'd heard this moment described by other women, but they hadn't done it justice. She squeezed her eyes tighter, and a keening escaped her in a wail. Brisa came for him, but he didn't let up.

"Ka'Sen!" she cried. "More!" Then she moaned a

long, unintelligible sound. Her hips jerked off the bed as she squealed with pleasure.

He replaced his tongue with a large finger but paused. "You're a virgin?"

She opened her eyes to look at him. He appeared shocked. Brisa scowled. "Of course. Why would you doubt that?"

He flushed. "Because I'm a fool. Forgive me." He kissed her again, and the frown creasing her brow relaxed. She kissed him back.

When he pulled away, she groaned with disappointment, but he returned his attention between her legs and used his tongue to build her need back into an inferno. He continued until she cried out, coming ferociously. He cupped her breasts tenderly, flicking her nipples with his thumbs as he watched her. His intense gaze made her feel both safe and exposed in the same moment. She couldn't pull away from the gravity in his expression, and he held her entranced as pleasure tingled through her.

He smiled. "Beautiful."

When she came back from the floating depths of ecstasy, she looked to see Ka'Sen kneeling between her legs. He dropped a kiss on her thigh. Her pussy contracted with the echoes of her orgasm. Even though she was a virgin, she knew they weren't done, and she wanted more.

His lust, almost palpable around them like some unseen entity, seemed to radiate into her. Brisa's want escalated with the desire in his expression. His passion made her hot. Her breath caught the moment his gaze captured hers. He trapped her on the mattress by placing his large hands on either side of her as he hovered over her. Her breathing grew shallow, and Ka'Sen groaned.

He rolled beside her, propping himself up on one arm so he could put his free hand between her legs. The sensation caused her to buck her hips and grind her clit against his touch. He chuckled. She bit her lip as her eyes fluttered closed, and a soft sound of pleasure escaped her.

He kissed her quickly and pulled back. "Amazing." He rubbed her clit while his index finger delved inside to caress her G-spot. Brisa whimpered as her desire sparked into flames. She pressed against him.

"What do you want?"

Her eyes opened. Their gazes locked. "More." Her vision hazed with lust.

He made a sound -- something between a moan and a growl. "Always look at me when you tell me what you want. You have beautiful eyes."

Brisa's face heated. She didn't look away. Prickles of awareness stirred in her womb, and her pussy responded. Her small fingers trailed lightly down his stubbled jaw. She put her hands on the back of his neck and pulled him to her lips. He choked out an emotional grunt and kissed her back with a ferocity that stole her thoughts. She lost her soul in him.

Ka'Sen cradled the right side of her face in his large, warm hand, and she turned into his palm, placing a tender kiss there. "I can feel your heart beating with my heart," he whispered.

She snuggled her cheek into his palm. He pressed his forehead against hers, and they sat there for a long moment. A strangely spiritual peace filled her.

Ka'Sen moved just enough to press a kiss against the crown of her head. "When you come, say my name." Then his lips descended into a punishing kiss.

She clung to him, breathless and wanting. She opened for his tongue to explore her mouth. No man had kissed her like this before. Her body reacted, and instinctually her tongue found his. He smothered her moans with his fervent kiss until her yearning erupted in flames.

Releasing her roughly, Ka'Sen put his mouth over her nipple, sucking hard. His hand slipped between her legs, strumming her clit. She bucked under him, writhing with the force of her lust.

Her heart thundered. Ka'Sen held her wrists against the mattress beside her head with one of his large hands while the other ran lightly down her torso. His gaze burned with an intensity that stole her breath. Heat rushed up her neck to blossom in her cheeks. He took her other arm, and pinned her under him. She was helpless, willingly helpless.

He continued to hold her in place. Brisa managed a half-hearted struggle until he spread her legs with his knee. The momentary feeling of violation rekindled her desire even as it brought a flash of panic to the surface of her emotions. Being imprisoned under him made her struggle out of pure instinct. Ka'Sen moved between her legs, holding her so that he could look down into her eyes. "I will not hurt you. Submit to me."

He was asking too much. She tried to tug free, but he was much stronger.

"Submit," he demanded. "I will release you when you are still. Remain as you are. Lock your fingers."

She stilled, but he didn't let go. They stared at each other for a moment. She tugged, just a little, and his grip tightened. Something uncoiled inside of her, and her pussy ached with need. Having him control her was something she'd never have thought she'd like, but she did. She didn't want him to stop. Biting her lip, she locked her fingers and held perfectly still.

They never broke eye contact. He grinned and brushed a gentle kiss against her lips. She bucked. "Please, Ka'Sen." She ground against him and rubbed her wet pussy against his thigh, crying out in frustration.

"Say the words," Ka'Sen ordered.

"I give in, whatever you want."

"That's not what I want." Ka'Sen kissed her neck until her pussy convulsed, and she groaned with pleasure.

"I'm yours," she panted. "I -- I need more," she gasped. She moaned, arching her back. "I want... inside... me... please!" Brisa cried out, not entirely sure what she begged for, just knowing she needed him.

"We become one," he said as his cock found her ready entrance. She gasped with surprise and squeezed her eyes shut as he slipped inside of her, stretching, violating, and then pain. He impaled her completely with a single thrust and pleasured grunt. The sting burned for a moment, yet the perfect fullness made the discomfort worthwhile. Her tension elevated.

He stilled, his body joined with hers. "It will be good again soon."

Ka'Sen let her go to find her clit, and he strummed her desire back to life. She closed her eyes and let herself stop thinking. Her hands found his ass, and she squeezed his perfection. He began moving inside her. Carefully, at first, and then with more force. He fit his fingers between them and managed to strum her clit even as he drove hard. She gasped, opening her eyes as she came.

"Ka'Sen," she cried, their bodies locked together,

and her ecstasy began again.

"You are mine!" he roared, moving inside her, throwing his head back. His face was taut. Orgasm rippled through her body, mind, and spirit. Her eyes fluttered closed again as a kaleidoscope of color exploded across her vision. Brisa shook with the force of her release. This was so much more than she'd ever dreamed. Her body responded to him without her conscious decision. She rocked against him, sliding him deeper inside of her. The beautiful friction caused intense tiny little wails of joy to erupt from her throat unhindered. Brisa allowed her body to become mindless sensation. Every single stroke of his cock brought a fresh spasm of pleasure through her. He was thrusting hard and fast, and he stroked her clit with his every move.

Brisa opened her eyes and gazed at Ka'Sen. His face twisted into a mask of concentration as he pumped inside of her, and she arched her back as Ka'Sen drove deeper. The pleasure didn't ebb. The ecstasy continued as the seconds became timeless. Nothing mattered but this man and his cock. A keening wail left her throat, and her breath hitched. Nothing in her experience had prepared her for this nirvana.

"You feel amazing," he muttered through his gritted teeth.

Carnality splintered through her, and she arched off his mattress. He stopped when he was deep inside her. Her pussy contracted instantly as her sensitivity peaked. She gripped him with her inner muscles as he thrust into her a final time. The heat of his seed filled her. He held her, and they shook from the power -- pleasure so intense it grew into something akin to pain. The sensation was so overwhelming her eyes watered.

"You were made for me," he whispered.

She wept, hard, sobbing with the uncontrollable expression of emotion. Ka'Sen held her and pushed the hair off her face. The smell of sex perfumed the air. He turned her head to the side, facing him, and smiled at her before placing a kiss to her mouth. He didn't let her pull away as he tugged her closer. They fit together perfectly. His body heat seeped into her soul. Her mind floated disconnectedly as her body indulged in the afterglow of mating.

"I've never felt this safe before," she whispered.

He flinched. Something unreadable passed over his face. "Enjoy that, because once you know me, you'll never say those words again."

"Why?" She genuinely wanted to understand.

He let go of her. She waited for a response. When one never came, she sat up to get out of bed. Ka'Sen snared her arm. "Where are you going?"

"My room."

His grip tightened. "You will stay here."

Brisa frowned. Realizing that returning to the servant's quarters wasn't a good option, and going to Val'Trea was unpredictable, she stayed. When she lay back, her husband put his arms around her and pulled her close. As suffocating as his embrace should have been, it was nice. Exhausted, she immediately drifted into oblivious slumber.

* * *

Ka'Sen held his wife close. He should want her to go. Enjoying the feel of her warmth had nothing to do with his quest for magic. Touching her was sorcery. Her words played over and over in his mind. *I've never felt this safe before*. That utterance ignited his pride and his wrath in equal measures. Someone had hurt her.

The idea of leaving her here undefended made him ill. He pulled her closer, and she mumbled unintelligibly in her sleep. Why she mattered to him was a mystery. He'd been with women far more beautiful. Her willing reluctance annihilated his resolve not to care about her. He'd imagined coming here, making a vow, mating, and then keeping her isolated in a comfortable room until the child was born.

His childhood pain rushed back. His mother's broken body haunted his nightmares. This time when his arms tightened around Brisa, she squeaked, and started to wake, but when he relaxed his grip, she drifted asleep again. He wouldn't harm her, even if the child were like him, with no magic. But she would keep giving him children until she gave him one with the gift.

He spent most of the night pondering how to convince her to come with him when he left. When he finally tumbled into a fitful sleep, his dreams were full of death.

* * *

Movement sprung Ka'Sen into defense mode. He pulled the saber from where he'd stashed it under the mattress and held it ready. His woman snuggled closer to him in sleep. He wasn't under attack. His cock stiffened as he caught the mingling scents of woman and sex. Dawn light filtered with a gray welcome into the room. He placed his weapon beside the bed, before slipping his hand under her head so he could pull her close for a morning kiss. She moaned against his lips, and that only made him want her more. For a moment, her eyes widened with confusion, then her face relaxed.

"Good waking," she said.

"Surprisingly so," he replied.

A soft flush stained her pale skin. Tousled brown hair curled at her temples to frame her face. He couldn't get enough of looking at her. So many women had thrown themselves at him, begging for his attention, but she didn't want him for who he was. That made what they shared last night the most genuine thing he'd ever experienced.

"Would you like to enjoy your breakfast alone or downstairs in the communal room with my father?"

"I'd like seconds of the delicious nectar I sampled last night," he murmured feeling lighter and more carefree than he had in a very long time. "I'll be having breakfast with you."

He rolled so that he pinned her against the plush mattress with his body. She gazed up at him, and he knew he'd have his way, in all things, with her. "I won't leave you here."

When Brisa opened her mouth to protest he closed it with a kiss. She wrapped her arms around his neck, and the welcome of her touch reached deep inside his soul. She soothed him, unlike anything he'd ever experienced. This place was so far removed from the battle for power he'd been born into. His purpose had never belonged to him, but lying in bed with this woman he could just be a man. There was a power in the simplicity he'd never imagined. He broke the kiss to gaze down into her big green eyes. His throat tightened as the magnitude of what she was to him left him awed. "You will come with me. Where I go. You go."

A frown marred her forehead, and she shook her head slightly in seemingly unconscious protest. "I wish I could, but I cannot. I am needed here. You agreed I could stay."

Ugly anger rose up, and he fought hard to hold back. The last thing he needed was to scare her, but she was his. He didn't give up his prizes. He'd taken whole worlds by force, but this one woman thought she could say no. And to his amazement, she could. He needed her compliant. Forcing a pregnancy, as was done to his mother, had proven fruitless in the conception of magic. "You promised me a child."

"I did." The heavy sorrow in her tone hurt him and made it harder to hold back the rage.

"You will give me a child."

"I will." Her eyes watered.

Physical pain gripped him. He pushed the hair off her forehead and kissed the single tear that trickled down. "Yes. You will, but I want something I didn't when I agreed to you staying. I want you to come with me, to raise this child with me. Be my wife in all ways." As the words tumbled out, he couldn't believe he was saying them, and worse, he couldn't believe he was pleading with her. "I will give you the universe. You'll never want for anything. I will protect you and our child. Be mine. I could force you -- will force you, but I don't want that. I want you in a way I've never wanted another. Give me your heart, don't make me take it." He had to make her understand. She had no choice. The only decision was to come as a beloved bride -- or a prisoner.

Her lower lip trembled, and he pressed his lips against hers, crushing her, dominating her. He'd show her how much she wanted him, make her want him. His cock hardened. Having her under him willing, but unwilling was intoxicating. He loved knowing that every sound of pleasure was a response to him, not his power. She made him more human than any other woman in the universe could.

He kept her pinned until she kissed him back. Her stiff body yielded under him. He reached between her legs and felt the slick desire. This woman was his. Her body knew it, even if her head needed convincing.

"I think I will fall in love with you," he whispered against her hair as if he had a choice.

She gasped. "You can't."

He chuckled. "I think you are the first bride in all the union worlds who would argue against her husband's love. What are you so afraid of?"

"Abandoning those who need me."

Her admission hit him in the pit of the stomach. He searched her gaze. Those beautiful green eyes were blind to his truth. "I need you. Your people still have your father. They also have the protection I can give them. You have no idea how special your planet is or how sacred. You are giving them unique security by staying at my side. If you stay here you won't have my ear, and they need you to have my ear. The decisions I make affect them in ways you've never considered. Do you know how powerful I am?"

"You're a prince. Princes have power. You can't scare me with threats."

He smiled, but the expression wasn't from joy. His eyes narrowed. "I never make threats, but I can promise bleakness. I can promise sorrow." To her credit, she didn't flinch. "Help me understand joy."

Instead of pulling away she wrapped her arms around him, pulling him close. He found his head resting on her shoulder in a wordless expression of comfort. Her cheek pressed against his warm skin. He was at a loss as to how to react, so he stiffened. She let go and turned away. "Sorry."

He had no idea what she was apologizing for, and pushed away the urge to beg for her touch again.

"The day lengthens. Let us rise."

Without a word she got up, grabbing a blanket and wrapping it around her nudity. She never looked back as she fled. Anger stirred, the kind that made him dangerous. He sat on the edge of the bed with his head in his hands for a long time. He never had to ask for anything so being with her put him out of his element. Used to planning military maneuvers, he wondered if the battle for her heart would always be so brutal. She made his heart bleed from a thousand invisible wounds.

He dressed in the black flight suit, which fit him perfectly. Being in his own clothing made him feel like himself again. He felt foolish for letting the female twist him up inside. She shouldn't have so much power over him.

A knock sounded on his door. He opened it and Rev stood there, agitated, nervous. "What's the matter with you?" Ka'Sen asked.

"Your bride isn't who you think she is, Kae. You've been tricked."

The darkest rage boiled inside of him. If Rosrel wanted a powerful enemy, it had one. "What do you mean?"

"I have to show you something."

Rev entered the room. Ka'Sen looked out into the hall before shutting the door. He could still smell his woman in the room. Whatever his friend had to show him he knew he was taking Brisa with him when he left. Without a doubt.

Command the Stars (Commanded 2)

Ashlynn Monroe

Ka'Sen, Prince of Planets, Leader of the Union of Worlds, can have anything he wants -- except magic. To get that power he must wed the princess of the only world with the fearsome force he craves. But when he takes his new wife into his bed he's bewitched by something more commanding than sorcery. Love.

Ka'Sen's never had the liberty to follow his emotions. Now that he knows his wife lied to him from the first moment they met, he definitely can't allow himself to trust in her or follow the vines of desire wrapping around his heart.

Brisa never dreamed she'd live in the beyond, traveling through the stars -- she also never imagined she'd be caught in a war between ideologies. Her new husband is a mystery of contradictions. So much about the wider universe is strange to her, but the feelings his nearness stirs are the strangest of all.

Hating this man should be so much easier than loving him. Interlopers in Ka'Sen's world beg her to save them, but doing so will destroy the only man she's ever loved. When she doesn't understand the game how can she possibly comprehend the stakes and know what's right?

Chapter One

Ka'Sen crossed his arms over his chest. He glared at his bodyguard, also his oldest friend, Reven. "What do you have to show me about my bride?"

Rev held out his digital.

As Ka'Sen crossed the room to accept the offered information, his feet ached with the chill. Outside, the morning air was cold, and the ancient stone walls did little to insulate against the coming winter. Old battle injuries protested. He'd crashed more than once. He'd experienced his share of hand-to-hand combat in the outer reaches of the empire, quelling rebel uprisings during his teens.

This world was apart from the rest of the empire, having rejected technology long ago, until now, when the king wanted modern weapons. Ka'Sen ran his hand through his hair. And that was why he was here, trading tech for magic. He wanted a dynasty of every kind of power.

The subtle hint of Brisa's perfume still lingered in the room. He'd much rather have been in the bed making love to his new bride, but when he saw Reven's screen he knew the honeymoon was over. He'd been married for less than a day, yet his wife already betrayed him.

She was not a princess.

"Are you sure?" Ka'Sen hoped Rev was wrong. "Where did you find this?"

"I sent a small group of investigators out when we landed. I apologize I didn't check with you first, but I didn't want my need to protect you to distract from the negotiations. We've been friends our entire life. Creating a legacy greater than your father's has motivated everything you've ever done. I know how important magic is to you, but this woman can't give you the child you need."

"They look identical." Almost. His bride had scars on her back and shoulders, but the woman in the picture did not. They could have been twins. Sisters surely. "Who did I marry?"

Rev rubbed the back of his neck and looked away. "I -- I'm trying to find out. How do we proceed?"

"I would consider this an act of war on any other world, but we have to tread carefully considering we won't be leaving without the king's blessing. The first thing we need to do is determine who by the gods I wed, then we decide how to get off this planet."

"And the woman?" Rev's eyebrow hiked up.

"We bring my bride home. We might still salvage this situation. I saw her use magic." Ka'Sen remembered how the king had looked at Brisa when Ka'Sen confronted him about having progeny in the village.

At the time, he'd worried Brisa was sleeping with a village boy. Now the moment held a layered significance. He let his memories wander back to the encounter. "*He's my -- brother. Father has had his share of trysts in the village,*" Brisa had said.

He might still have the king's daughter's hand, just not the daughter he'd planned to take. Her royal status mattered little to him. Her power was what he craved, and now more than that he wanted her -- her body -- maybe even her heart.

He'd been her first lover, so the boy he'd grown angry over hadn't taken what was his. But the locals still knew something about Brisa.

"Princess Val'Trea is certainly not well loved, but

feared." Rev scowled. "I am not having much luck finding out her secrets. Without technology, I'm failing you."

"Brisa!"

"What?" Rev squinted as if narrowing his focus would help him understand his prince's outburst.

"She asked me to call her Brisa. Also, there was a boy. Fair-haired. Gangly. I believe he might have answers for us."

"I will find him." Rev promised and rushed out.

Ka'Sen growled out a sound of rage as he slammed his fist into a wooden cabinet, obliterating the polished antiquity with a single thrust.

Neff, one of his trusted guards, rushed in. "Highness?"

"Leave me." Ka'Sen struggled to calm the turmoil in his soul. She'd given him a moment of peace, but that joy kindled in his heart only to burn his psyche to ash.

Neff paused as if he wanted to speak, but then turned, shutting the door behind him. Ka'Sen dressed in his own clothing, a black flight suit that fit him like a second skin, then pulled on his boots and gathered his things. If he'd just brought a med tech down with him they'd have DNA assurance his suspicion about Brisa was right. She had magic in her. He felt it. A magic she would pass down to his child -- or children. Magic that would ensure his legacy.

He left the room, and his guards followed him at a close distance. Servants bowed and shrank back from him as he trudged along in a single-minded pursuit of truth. He imagined how fierce he appeared to these primitives, but worry about the future stole his compassion. He didn't try to soften his appearance, even after one of the young maids burst into tears when he met her eyes.

* * *

Brisa stood, shaking, as the king glowered at her. "I should have you executed. When this is over I will decide your punishment." He never said a word about Val'Trea and what her punishment would be. Likely, whatever it was, Brisa would bear the burden of that too.

"Father," Val'Trea said. "Brisa did as I asked. I have saved us from giving those in the beyond magic. You get your weapons, and we keep our magic. We even keep dear Brisa. I fail to see why you are so angry."

Only Val'Trea would be able to tell the king how right her wrongness was with such bold skill. The ruler's face mottled scarlet and his eyes bulged. Brisa shuddered as he turned his wrath in her direction. "You! You!" was all he managed to sputter. Sweat beaded on his upper lip and brow.

"Your majesty, your heart," cried out Sir Hae'Far, the king's faithful advisor. "The doctor has warned against sudden bouts of rage."

Brisa dropped to her knees before the king. "I have done the bidding of my mistress, and I have kept my identity secret. He -- he was kind with me, Majesty, but I would never betray you."

King Vel'Spei's eyes narrowed, and his mustache twitched as his lip curled. "You have already betrayed me."

Brisa flinched. She looked down at her feet. Emotion tightened her throat painfully.

"Oh, Father, do calm down. You're making poor Hae'Far wet himself. He isn't looking forward to a world without your protection. Brisa hasn't done anything to betray us. She's been a good and faithful servant to me -- and to you. Please, Father." Val'Trea ended with a pleading inflection, and she went over to where her father sat, fell to her knees, and put her cheek against this hand. "Don't be angry."

"I just don't understand." Vel'Spei pulled away from his daughter, lifting his arms in the air, and looked up, shaking his hands. His ruddy cheeks grew redder. "Why would you risk our entire kingdom to keep magic away from those in the beyond? We aren't giving it to every world. We are giving it to one man and creating a powerful alliance of houses -- worlds. It's time we stepped out of the past to embrace the future."

Val'Trea frowned as she gazed up at her father. She even batted her long, dark lashes and wore the most beguiling of innocent expressions. "What kind of future will we have when those from the beyond don't fear us anymore? They will come, and they will destroy us."

The king's eyes narrowed. "You are not an altruistic girl." He paused, and leaned toward his kneeling daughter. "What is in this for you?"

"I don't understand."

His brows drew closer together. "You do. And you *will* tell me." He grabbed Val'Trea's chin, squeezing so hard his arm shook. Rage blazed in his eyes.

Fear rooted Brisa to the spot, and her breath caught as she watched the princess gaze unflinchingly at her father. A cunning smile twitched for a moment on Val'Trea's lips. "Power."

The king let her go with a jerk. "Power?"

She nodded, and this time the smile remained steadfast. "Power. If I remain pure I will master death.

I will be legendary -- the most feared woman who has ever lived. I will be the goddess."

"Sacrilege," Brisa hissed.

They turned to her, and she slapped her hands over her mouth. She stood on shaking legs.

Val'Trea stretched out her hand. Rapid utterances came from the princess in a soft, albeit menacing tone. Brisa shrieked as an unseen force pushed her back, her legs stretched out uselessly as her heels dragged across the marble floor. She hit the wall hard enough to knock the wind out of her, and there she dangled.

Turning to her father, the princess kept her hand up. "As you can see, I am beyond the parlor tricks of your tutors. Give me my freedom, and I will give you this world. I am the only weapon you need. Why do you think those in the beyond are so desperate for magic? It -- this ability -- can be so very much more. We've stopped striving for what our ancestors found when we took magic away from the common people. Lazy. Wasteful. I am more than a marriage contract."

Val'Trea locked her gaze with her father's, and he seemed to study Val'Trea's face. After what felt like an eternity, he nodded. "And do you believe you are powerful enough to prevent an attack if the sky prince discovers your treachery?"

Val'Trea shrugged. "He won't."

She dropped her arm, and Brisa collapsed to the floor. Even in her fear and pain, Brisa was stunned at the princess's confident audacity.

Vel'Spei turned to Brisa, not his daughter. "He'd better not. He'd better not."

"I will not tell him. I just want to stay here and protect what's important to me."

The king's brow arched. "What is important to

you?"

"The orphans. And those in the village."

Seemingly satisfied, Vel'Spei nodded. "Make sure you remember how important your silence is, then. I will reward you if we are successful."

The door banged against the wall as it flew open. Brisa flinched as she saw Ka'Sen and his guards enter. They wore expressions of righteous rage. Pain etched her husband's face, and it tore at her soul. She wanted to go to him, but how could she when she was no one to him.? Helplessness like she'd never suffered before rolled through her as she tried not to cry.

When his gaze passed over Brisa, her throat tightened until it hurt. It was as if he didn't see her. This was the closest to being dead she'd ever been, and his inability to recognize her hurt her heart.

"Vel'Spei, I am taking my bride and leaving."

The king stood. His gaze lingered on his daughter a second before he scowled at Ka'Sen. "You will not." Even aging and portly, he still managed a commanding presence.

Brisa kept her gaze focused on the princess to keep from having to look at the man she'd betrayed. Her heart hurt, and her arms ached to hold him. As angry and confused as she was, nothing mattered when she remembered his touch. An involuntary shudder ran through her. His head snapped in her direction, but she continued to look away.

"I will have what is mine," Ka'Sen said in a cold, even tone. "I will take Brisa when I leave."

The king and princess both glared at her. Vel'Spei recovered first. He turned to Ka'Sen. "Explain yourself."

Ka'Sen scowled. "I've never been asked to explain myself, but as you are by contract my father-in-law, I will. You didn't give me your daughter, as promised. You gave me a servant."

He turned to Brisa, and her heart broke. She stared at him this time, unable to pull her gaze away. He was like water in the desert, and when he looked at her like that she grew thirsty. She didn't realize she'd licked her lips until he grinned. "This is my wife." He pointed at her -- her -- and she stopped breathing. "Mine." And she gulped down a breath. "Another man might kill you for such an insult, but I feel... generous... and I accept my bride. We will leave without retaliation, but Brisa comes with me."

Vel'Spei nodded. "I could kill you, or force you to remain, but you have been dishonored. Take the woman and leave as our friend, providing you supply me with the weapons."

"The agreed-upon gift will be here shortly. We will give you what we promised and leave with my wife. She may not be a princess, but she may well be your daughter. Do you deny her?"

"I do not. Go in peace, but remember my generosity. Leave as my ally, as family. Brisa is dear to my household."

She had to give the king credit for his ass-covering skills. "But... he agreed to leave his wife here."

All eyes turned to her.

Ka'Sen's grin widened. "I agreed to leave the princess here. There was nothing said about you, sweet Brisa. You will come home with me."

Her mouth went dry. "This is my home."

"Where I am, you will be at home."

His words were far more ominous than she'd expected. Her breath caught as her knees trembled. "Please. Show me mercy."

His grin was so wide, he appeared frighteningly manic. "You will forget mercy under my control. I will possess you -- completely. You will beg for more."

She didn't doubt he'd make good on his threat. Trepidation filled her. She looked around, praying for some sign she could save herself, but nothing appeared. "There are people here who need me. If you have no mercy for me, then grant it to them."

His nostrils flared as his eyes narrowed. "What would you give me to keep them safe?"

"I have nothing."

A sly grin curved the left side of his mouth. "You hold far more value than you think."

"Whatever you want. Take whatever you need."

His brows drew together. "You have no idea what you're agreeing to." He frowned. "What I want I cannot take."

She tried to understand until he grabbed her shoulders. She gasped. "Don't hurt me."

Anger crossed his expression. "Those who you so casually offer everything to protect, who are they?"

"Orphans."

"Orphans?"

She nodded.

Ka'Sen laughed hard, genuine amusement made him shake with the force of his mirth. He let go of her shoulders.

Immediate rage bubbled up. She glared at him, insulted to her core, but not sure why she stood in silence.

"Orphans. I should have expected something that ridiculous."

She jerked, slapped by the force of his cruelty. "The lives of children are not ridiculous."

His expression took on a hard intensity. "Yes.

They are." He turned to the King. "Would you see that her orphans are cared for in exchange for more weapons?"

The king's mouth dropped. He nodded mutely.

"Excellent. If I were to find out you have lied, we would no longer be allies. I would want regular correspondence regarding these orphans. If you are so kind I would like to take one or two with us as well. That way Brisa would not feel so alone in her new home."

Vel'Spir nodded. "Agreed."

"Where are your orphans?" Ka'Sen asked Brisa.

"The village, the old temple."

Ka'Sen turned to one of his guards. "Go. Bring back two of them, the two that appear to need a good meal the most."

"They're -- ill." She turned to Val'Trea. "When will they be well? I've done my part of our bargain."

Ka'Sen glared at Brisa and her stomach rolled. "So. You've been protecting your orphans?" He turned to the princess. "I could use someone so soulless as one of my commanders. You missed your calling."

Val'Trea appeared pleased. "I have a destiny here. But thank you for seeing what my dear father has always overlooked." She paused before moving toward Brisa, who took a step back.

Ka'Sen moved between them.

The princess's eyes shone with unshed tears. "I will miss you. If you are my sister, you've been far better to me than I have to you. Your littles are well, and I will make sure Father keeps his word, because you have saved me."

Brisa managed to nod, but as contrary as Val'Trea could be, Brisa was afraid to speak. Leaving the powerful witch feeling generous was the safest for her orphans so she didn't say the many things that lingered on her tongue.

"Take Brisa to the ship. When Reven and the children arrive we take off, so begin the cycle. Make sure the fusion port is secure. We had trouble with it during landing."

A big man, dark and strong, took her by the arm. Fear caused Brisa to struggle, until she looked over at Ka'Sen. Something in his posture made her relax. He wouldn't let this massive male hurt her.

A sense of helplessness filled her as they moved down the corridor. She didn't have much, but they had left her sleeping space so quickly she hadn't had time to gather her basket. "Please let me get my things."

The guard stopped. He pressed something metallic at his wrist. "Shall I honor her request?"

Ka'Sen's voice drifted from nothing. "Ten minutes."

She gasped.

The guard grinned. "You haven't seen anything yet. Which way?"

She pointed toward the kitchen. He followed her. Behind the cooking fire she had her blanket and a basket of random things her littles had made for her over the years. She had an assortment of Val'Trea's cast-off dresses too, but she didn't want to take those and begin her new life in her nemesis's hand-me-downs.

"Is that everything?"

She nodded.

"I wish my woman packed as light." He pressed the metallic device on his wrist again. "ETA five minutes."

She let him drag her out of the castle as she clutched her few possessions. A craft, sleek and silver, waited on the lawn. A horse whinnied and shied away from the strange transport. She'd seen these, in drawings at the temple, but she'd never dreamed she'd be riding in one. This kind of technology was an abomination. She closed her eyes. "Forgive me, dear goddess. Protect me."

The guard had to tug her harder. "Come on," he coaxed.

"Is -- is it safe?"

"I was born on a transport not much bigger than that. It's safe."

"You were born in space?"

"I was."

"How did the goddess find you for your first blessing?"

His reply was a throaty chuckle.

She watched the odd craft open and with a little encouragement she allowed the guard to lead her inside. The place smelled unnatural, chemical. She took a step back and bumped into the wall. "I -- I don't belong here."

"You will. Welcome to the real world."

"What are you called?"

He gave a bark of laughter. "Things a sweet girl like you shouldn't hear, but for the sake of naming, you may call me Blaze."

"Blaze?"

He nodded. "Buckle up."

She sat down, yelping as something metallic snaked up over her lap. It cinched and pulled her snuggly back into her seat. She dropped her basket and blanket as she pushed at the belt, struggling.

"Automated. Don't worry, it's for safety. You're all right."

Blaze's assurance wasn't enough. She still fought

the automated prison until the door opened with a hiss. Her attention jerked to the entrance. Her new husband boarded, and behind him Reven carried Hoda and Boris over his shoulders. Both children flailed.

When the door closed Reven set the children on their feet. They stopped crying the moment they saw her. Boris reached for Brisa, his little hands clenching and unclenching in reflexive terror. Hoda wiped her eyes. Brisa opened her arms, and they ran to her. She hugged them tight. "Where were you?" Hoda whispered.

"I'm sorry." She stroked the bangs off the girl's face.

Boris began sucking his thumb. She was so glad these were the two children they'd picked. Hoda was like a little sister. In fact, Brisa suspected the child was another of the king's bastards.

Boris was the youngest, a beautiful child with big blue eyes and dark hair. He'd been about three years old when Lee, her dearest friend, had discovered the boy bleeding in a ditch. He'd never spoken. No one knew who he was or where he'd come from, so Boris stayed. She'd named him herself, picking something strong and hoping he could grow into the moniker. He'd been with them two years and had never said a word.

Brisa cupped his cheek. "Boris, sit here." She patted the empty seat next to her. He sat, and she held his hand as the lap belt strapped him in, as well.

Brisa pointed to the seat across from her. "Hoda." The girl sat, and their fingers touched until the restraints also held her tight. She glanced up at Ka'Sen. "Thank you." He nodded, taking the seat next to Hoda. The girl scooted away from him as much as she could.

Reven and Blaze went to the front of the craft and took positions at the controls. She watched in fascination as they manipulated the touchscreen panel until lights flashed and blinked.

Boris sucked his thumb louder. Hoda turned awkwardly, watching. "I hope they've done that before," Hoda whispered far too loudly.

The child's mutter made Ka'Sen grin. Something about the moment twisted Brisa's heart. He'd been such a skilled, caring lover. If he could learn to be a kind man, as well, she could love him.

Chapter Two

Brisa's fingers dug into the arms of her seat as the machine came to life. The thunderous noise and shaking sent both children into a fit of screaming. She struggled to contain her urge to join them.

"Quiet!" Ka'Sen barked, and his deep scowl immediately silenced the terrified children.

"There's no need to be harsh with them." Brisa let go of her seat's arm and clutched the hand Boris wasn't sucking on for both her comfort and his. "This isn't something they've ever endured, nor have I. We are all afraid."

Ka'Sen's scowl deepened. He settled back in his seat. "There is nothing to fear."

Brisa made eye contact with Hoda. "All is well. This is an adventure we are on together." She kept her tone light, albeit firm. Squeezing Boris's hand, she looked over to him. "I will not let you be harmed. I would protect you both with my life."

The sense of being watched made her turn her head. Ka'Sen was gazing at her with an unreadable expression. His look was almost wistful. She gave him a small smile, meaning to be encouraging, or at the least comforting. The shock of her predicament was still lingering, but she had enough of her wits to realize this was not a situation he'd been prepared for, either, and he, too, was off-balance. They were all in this together now, but the prince held their futures hostage.

Her mouth was dry. The craft darkened, and she held her breath. Tears rolled down Hoda's cheeks, but she remained quiet.

Brisa's heart swelled with pride. "We're in space."

Boris's eyes widened. He began sucking his thumb with impressive ferocity.

"Boy." Ka'Sen's voice held a softer note. "If you look straight up you'll see the stars."

They all looked up at a small round window above them.

Brisa gasped. "It's so beautiful."

"Yes, beautiful," Ka'Sen agreed. When Brisa glanced at him he wasn't looking up. He was looking at her. She felt her cheeks warm. For a moment, their gazes stayed locked before she turned away.

The children were calm now -- Boris had even stopped sucking his thumb -- and they all settled back. "I never thought I would ever travel in space," Hoda whispered. She cringed away from Ka'Sen as if she were afraid he'd hit her.

He frowned. "I will not hurt you. You may speak, but do so quietly."

Hoda seemed to relax and looked about the craft with a curious expression. *Curiosity*. There was so much they didn't know. There was so much Brisa needed to know. "Why did you take us? My littles are innocent. They don't deserve to be pawns in a game they can't win."

Ka'Sen shrugged. "You're my wife."

"Technically, but --"

"But nothing," Ka'Sen interrupted. "You are mine." He looked at the children. "And they will ensure you have a reason to be obedient."

She flinched as if he'd just slapped her. "Obedient?"

"I need a child. You will give that to me. You may already carry my offspring."

Her hot cheeks only added to her embarrassment as she glanced at where the other men sat. They didn't seem to be paying attention. "Shh."

"There is no shame in this. You. Are. My. Wife. For today and for always, I claim you as mine."

Her pulse raced. There was something delightfully primal in his claim that spoke to everything inside her that made her a woman. "I know nothing about you," she protested weakly.

"Is Brisa your real name?"

Maybe he knew less about her than she assumed. "Yes, my name is Brisa. As a bastard I have no more than that to claim. I was given a common name because I am common. I've served Princess Val'Trea as her lady maiden since I was old enough to understand the role. I was abandoned on the castle door step as an infant. I was lucky to have such a good position."

"You're of the royal line." He glanced at Hoda. "This one too. Your coloring and bone structure gives away your heritage in that noble house. I don't care which side of the blanket you were born on, but I do care that you have magic. I saw you use it."

She bit her lip.

"In the forest, with the flower, your offering to your goddess. I found you interesting."

She didn't know if she should be as offended as she felt. "*Interesting*? Am I still *interesting*?"

"Very."

"What happens to me when I stop being interesting? Just promise me the children will never be harmed."

"Their happiness is in your hands."

"I would never want to walk away from a child. Would you take an infant from my arms?"

"No. Not unless you opposed the legacy I would gift my son."

"What if it's a girl?"

"Or daughter. I ask you to join me as my wife in all ways. There is much about the vast expanse of this universe you won't understand, but trust me that what I do, I do for the greater good."

There was something ominous in his tone, and a chill slithered down her spine. She shivered.

He took a small tank and mask from under his chair. "You have one too. The change between recycled air and fresh air may make you feel ill. Put this over your head and press the green button." He demonstrated.

Brisa was glad he'd misinterpreted her physical reaction. She didn't want the children to grow ill so she put the masks from under their seats on them before putting on her own. They all sat silently, breathing in the more concentrated oxygen. She was glad for the forced silence. He'd given her a lot to think about before they arrived in his domain.

* * *

Ka'Sen felt the subtle bump, then click, of the shuttle catching the ship's dock. The children and his woman all appeared apprehensive again. He hadn't expected them to be so skittish. It was hard to imagine a world free from the daily conveniences he took for granted.

His bride's eyes were wide. He hadn't handled this well. She'd end up as traumatized as his mother had been if he wasn't careful. Pushing those dark memories away, he focused on Brisa's face. He wouldn't let that happen to the mother of his child. He would surpass his father in all ways, including love.

As he took off his mask he noticed her hands shaking. "Damn the gods."

She took off hers. "What?"

The safety belts disengaged. "Nothing. Gather your things and follow me." How could he explain how tenuous everything was without scaring her more? He needed her to accept her new role as fast as possible. Telling her how close to war they were would only scare her more. She'd left one world on the brink of revolt only to join another with *worlds* ready to dethrone the king. As heir to that throne he'd do anything to protect his future.

Brisa helped the children take off their masks before picking up her scattered belongings. She stood, and followed Ka'Sen. Reven took the children's hands. They kept glancing back at Brisa. She nodded, and this seemed to reassure her young ones.

"The orphans can stay together in Level C, but my wife will share my room." Ka'Sen held Brisa's hand firmly when she tried to pull away to follow her littles, as she called them.

"Brisa!" Hoda cried.

"It will be okay. I'll come to you as soon as I can." She turned back to Ka'Sen, glaring. "Why are we being separated?"

"It will be easier for them to settle in without you. Let them get used to their new home. You will not be able to be with them constantly. As my wife, you'll have responsibilities."

"Oh, yes, the baby-making." Sarcasm dripped from her words.

Ka'Sen turned to Reven. "Go. I will comfort my woman. See that the children are calm and happy. Show them the vids. Kids love those."

Reven laughed. "I bet you kids have never seen a talking hippopotamus."

"What's a hipp-a-mouse?" Hoda asked. Boris sucked his thumb until it pruned.

Slapping his hands together, Reven rubbed them fast in an excited gesture. "You just wait and see, little lady. You'll love it. Harry Hippo is the best creature in all the worlds. He's my favorite."

Hoda's brow wrinkled, but she let Reven take her hand. His enthusiasm won her over. Hoda held out the other hand to Boris. "I will look after you," she promised. The three of them left the room, and the door swished shut with a soft noise.

Brisa let out the breath she'd unconsciously held.

"They will be fine." Ka'Sen grinned. "And yes, the baby-making, and showing your support by standing at my side. You have much to prepare for to truly be my wife. There is much for you to learn, but the first lesson is that I control everything. All that happens on this ship, and on every inhabited planet in our federation, happens only with my permission. My family saved the worlds once, and I keep order to ensure humanity will never stand on the precipice of extinction again."

She crossed her arms over her chest. "And who gives you the right to decide what is order?"

He paused. She challenged him already, not a good sign. "This ship, Vulture, is the most advanced biomechanical weapon in space. My power gives me all the permission I need to stay in control."

"What if I don't agree with your definition of order? Would you destroy me?"

"I might not have the magic your princess used to control you, but I do have two of your orphans. Don't test me. I have no desire to hurt those small ones, but if you push me I will not fall over easily. I do not accept defeat, so if you choose to live a war expect to lose. The children will take the weight of your disobedience."

Her eyes narrowed, and her lips thinned. Even angry she was beautiful. He wanted her to bend to his needs and welcome him into her arms. The first night she'd been his wife had been the most at peace he'd ever been.

"Tell me what you want from me? Truly, what will my life here be?"

"Much of that is up to you. I ask you to be in my bed, as you were last night. I ask you to take your meals with me. The rest of your time is up to you."

Her lips parted, but her brows drew together. "You really want me in your bed."

Her innocence and stubborn pride were a heady aphrodisiac. His cock hardened. He couldn't stop his smile. "You have no idea how much." He'd been with women all over the galaxy, but this one woman intrigued him more than even the most skilled courtesan. And that irritated the hell out of him because she was the only person who could steal his dream.

"Stop glaring at me," she demanded.

"I wasn't," he lied.

"The children need me."

"All over the galaxy there are orphans. These two children are nothing special."

Her eyes narrowed to slits. "They are to me!"

He admired her devotion. She'd be a lioness protecting his children, and something about the idea of her holding his heir made his heart beat faster. There was promise in his image of her. A promise that she would be everything he needed -- everything his legacy needed. "Then they are to me, as well. We will care for them, but tonight you will let me fill you with my seed. You will give my line magic."

She gasped as he grabbed her and pushed her

against the wall. He hated her fear, but he needed it. He ran his hand down her arm, feeling the delicate pebbling of goose bumps. She shivered. He grinned. She was ripe for plucking, and he was ready to harvest her bounty.

The fear flickered out of her expression as anger took over. "You might control the whole galaxy, but you don't dictate my heart. If you want that, you'll earn it."

He glared at her. He'd expected resistance, but not strategy. She was more than he deserved. Taming her was a worthy use of his time, providing he planted the seeds of his dynasty in her womb. Holding her in place, he let her anger seep into him, and he closed his eyes against the rush as her rage tingled through him. He could feel her power, and he'd teach her obedience to use everything she was only for him.

He took a restraint clip from the utility belt at his waist. For a second, he hesitated. She was his wife, and this wouldn't look good, but teaching her she belonged to him was more important that the opinions of those who might see them. He was the prince -- the future king. She would learn that what he wanted was all that mattered. And he wanted to teach his woman complete obedience. She didn't struggle, and he realized she had no idea what he was going to do as he clipped her left wrist. Her mouth rounded into an *O*, and her brows drew together as he clicked the cuff in place, quickly repeating the process on her right.

He'd teach her to protect herself from everything except him.

* * *

The restraints bit into her skin. Brisa whimpered, but not from fear. Something stirred within her, and it was the strangest sensation. Darkness and light twined around her essence, binding her with misery's barbed wire to his spirit.

"You are mine. Come," he demanded and led her out of the shuttle and onto the ship. Afraid to resist, she let Ka'Sen lead her into his world.

His ship was so bright her eyes ached, and she squinted as he pulled her down corridor after corridor. All of them were the same shades of beige, silver, and white. The ship smelled of sanitation. There were no nature smells, no animal odors, just the sameness over and over as he tugged her along. The artificial light was irritating, and everything looked so flat, so wrong. Panic welled up, and the need for fresh air became almost overwhelming.

He paused. "Are you ill?"

"I -- I need -- space."

"You have it. Look out the port window."

She turned in the direction he pointed. It was beautiful. The stars surrounded a blue-and-green orb. "Is that -- home?"

"Yes. Beautiful. That is your world. It looks small from here, and I want you to think about that. You are not losing a home, you're gaining a universe. Let me give you everything."

Everything? It was a lot to consider, but the sight of her world from the great beyond calmed her, and she managed to catch her breath. He ran a hand down her arm. She shivered because through the thin fabric she could feel the heat of his skin. She'd worn her most serviceable working dress this morning because she hadn't want him to realize she was the woman he'd married, but when he touched her she realized they were connected by more than what they could see. The thread of magic hung between them.

A large group of men wearing uniforms like Reven's marched past. A man, a man with three eyes, struggled between them. She turned to gawk at their backs.

"Halt!" Ka'Sen shouted. He turned to her. "Stay here." Then he marched over to the group of soldiers. "What's this man's infraction?"

The one with more icons on his chest gave a brisk nod and bowed to Ka'Sen. "Spy, my prince. Caught him transmitting codes to Well Water. Taking him to the air lock to jettison the traitor."

"So you've caught and executed his conspirators on the ground?" Ka'Sen crossed his arms over his chest.

"No, but --"

"But nothing," Ka'Sen said sharply, glowering at the man. He went over to the prisoner and grabbed his earlobe. The three-eyed man howled the most painful cry she'd ever heard. Brisa would have covered her ears if her hands weren't bound. "Tell me who helped you?"

"I will die first," gasped the captive. "May the gods eat your soul."

"They will dine on yours first, if you don't give up your conspirators. They will be found with or without your suffering." Ka'Sen motioned his men forward. "Take him to my father for interrogation. He'll break, or he'll die, but we won't waste this opportunity."

Brisa shuddered. She always made herself scarce during judgments and never saw the king dispense a punishment. She knew there were executions, but she avoided that sorrowful activity as much as she could. She'd been told by the priestess some people were created by the goddess as sensitive -- empathic -- and she was one of those few. She'd been warned that she would experience the pain of others more deeply. The man's resolve radiated through her. He would die. He was someone's child, husband, or father. It hurt her so much to imagine the pain his family would endure. She swiped at a tear with the back of her bound hand.

"Don't," Ka'Sen ordered. "Don't give that worthless dissident your attention. He committed suicide the moment he stepped onto the Vulture. Come."

She hated his tone, which reminded her of someone calling a dog. Still, she obeyed.

Ka'Sen led her farther into his domain. She experienced a suffocating moment of claustrophobia when they stepped into a conveyance he called the elevator. How long would it be until she felt sun or a breeze on her skin? Her stomach clenched, but she fought and won control over the topsy-turvy sensation of the walls closing in on her. He brought her out into another identical hall, and after more twists and turns he stopped in front of a door. It didn't appear special. "A-724. This is my -- our -- cabin. This is where you will live with me as my wife."

Her heart pounded. He entered a code into the panel, then pressed her hand against the scanner. It beeped as a light danced up and down under her skin.

"Now you can enter and exit as you please. I want this to be your home. I want this to be a happy place for you, and for our child." His gaze fell on her stomach, and she flinched.

He picked her up, and she let out a little shriek. "Old custom," he explained as he carried her over the threshold to their room. Once inside he set her on her feet.

There was a large bed against the interior wall.

She saw an open doorway with what appeared to be his privy. On the other side of the room was a table and a very plush, long seat. A large section of the wall moved, and she stepped closer. Fish. The image of various water creatures swam around on the wall. They looked so real. She reached out, the weight of her restraint made it difficult to touch, but she brushed the tips over her fingers over the smooth surface.

"If you don't care for fish I can set it to display nature scenes when we aren't watching something. There is much I need you to learn from vids, but tonight the learning takes place on my bed, and only my bed. Take off your dress."

She held up her bound wrists. "That might be a little hard for me to do right now." Panic at his abrupt expectation made her glance at the door. If she ran, where would she hide? She didn't want her littles to suffer for her lack of courage.

He nodded. "I see." In a few powerful strides he was across the room, using his thumbprint to release the cuffs, and then she was free. He pushed the hair off her face before he dipped down, kissing her with a ravenous yet somehow angry caress of his lips. His aggression didn't surprise her, but the underlying tenderness left her confused. His mouth ignited a hunger in her.

Brisa wanted to rip his clothes off and see the hard strength outlined through the fabric of his flight suit. Awash in a tidal wave of desire her breath puffed out in little pants. When he pulled back she gazed into his eyes. His expression said he could read her soul, and that comforted her just as much as the idea terrified her. He owned her in a way she didn't know anyone could. The cuffs on her wrists were nothing compared to the way he'd captured her soul. He'd bought her with his naked sorrow. She wanted to make him whole because maybe… just maybe… healing him would fix the fissure of loneliness that split her psyche.

She was tired. The long hurt in her heart had worn her down. She just wanted to feel -- anything -- more than empty. He had filled her with more than his cock on their wedding night, and she closed her eyes, enjoying his scent like the primal thing she was deep down. Lust, to her embarrassment, made her needy for his hard body. What would the goddess think of her passion for this heathen roaming the stars?

It didn't matter. She couldn't deny she craved him.

This time, she wanted the joining to be more than quick and angry. He made the magic inside her spark to life. The buzz in her deepest darkness sang with a power that promised more. She let her attention linger on that growing pulse of energy. Her throat ached with the need to hold back the magnitude of what he could do to her body.

Not only did he give her pleasure, he made her stronger. With that strength she experienced a terrible mystery she didn't understand how to control, but release was so wonderful she craved the risk. She should want to run from him, but instead she was drawn into his flame. He could burn her to nothing if she wasn't careful.

He leaned forward, and lips brushed together ever so slightly until he pressed his firmly to hers. Only his mouth touched her, and she longed for freedom. She'd throw her arms around him and hold him close. She'd never let him go -- but restrained, she was at his mercy. She wanted more, but he taunted her with distance. She couldn't blame him.

He broke the kiss, moving to the curve of her

neck, sucking hard until she hung in his arms. Her eyes pressed tight, and she moaned, grinding against him shamelessly. Her pussy throbbed, growing wet, as she tried to get some friction against his thigh, but he moved back, leaving her feeling frustrated. She ached for release.

Which he provided, but it was the cuffs at her wrists, not her orgasm, he freed. The cuffs clattered to the floor.

"I'm -- tainted," she breathed against his lips.

Ka'Sen pulled away and looked down into her face. "No. You are exquisite. I want you. You know I want to join with you again, now."

A frisson of excitement ran through Brisa. "I know."

"And." His eyes grew as dark as his tone was foreboding. "There will be no one else -- ever. I do not share what is mine."

The energy between them was unstable, and a feral need radiated from him. She should be horrified, but instead the obsession lurking below the surface of his emotions fueled her own desire. She swallowed. "Yes." Her throat tightened, but she managed to respond.

He gazed down into her face with his mixture of savage and sorrow. "Yes what?"

Giving him what he wanted should be like ash in her mouth. Each syllable only sparked to ignite the ache melting her core and leaving her wetness a constant reminder of how much her body betrayed her mind. "Yes, husband."

Brisa licked her dry lips. Strange, but saying the words didn't hurt like they should. This man -- monster -- hurt people, threatened her littles, and yet there was something good in him. She just had to reach it.

Unable to help herself, she reached up and brushed a lock of his dark hair from his eyes. He needed a haircut. He didn't pull away at her touch, but there was a hard challenge in his eyes, as if she had the power to hurt him. The very idea was so ridiculous she chuckled.

"What amuses you, wife?"

"Us. This. What have you done to me?"

A seductive grin curved his full lips. "You're the one with magic. Shouldn't I be asking that question?" His head dipped down, and he kissed her before she could respond, effectively scattering her thoughts so her glib reply fled her mind. Her arms wrapped around his neck, and she let herself belong to him in this space for the moments they kissed.

His groan sent a flutter through her core and caused her to press closer to him. She wanted to be filled with him. Craving the connection only he could give her made her clutch him tighter. He brought his hands up, cupping the sides of her face, and kissing her with desperation so visceral her heart beat faster.

She pulled away. "How can you want me?"

Chapter Three

Ka'Sen stared. She had to be kidding. Keeping her in agony took every ounce of his self-control. She had no idea how much he wanted her, and he needed the situation to remain like that. If she had any idea how much command she had over him he'd lose everything. He needed her confusion, or his dream was lost. "Take off your dress," he ordered.

Slack-jawed, she gaped at him. "Don't I get a tour of the ship first?"

"Delaying tactics will not work. I need what only you can give me."

"Bread? I bake the best bread in the castle."

He grinned. "Buns, specifically one in your oven. I'm not playing games with you Brisa. You *are* my wife, and you *will* birth my child."

"Your bedroom seduction needs work. This conversation is far from romantic."

He shrugged. "You strike me as more of a practical woman than a romantic. Am I wrong?"

"In many ways, you are right, but about this you are very wrong."

Ka'Sen didn't agree, but he remained quiet. Anyone willing to sacrifice their virginity to save a bunch of orphaned children had a big heart. People with large hearts tended to look at the big picture and focus on the greater good, leaning heavily toward the practical spectrum. He doubted his wife was an exception. She was a virtual stranger. He knew her body -- well -- but not her heart. "You are mine."

"I'm not the wife you thought you married. I'm no princess."

Ka'Sen shook his head, astonished at her lack of

vision. "As my wife you are empress of worlds. I am not unhappy with the outcome of your sister's treachery and your father's cowardice."

"The king might not be my father. I could be an ordinary peasant."

"Your pedigree doesn't matter to me. We both know you have magic, and there's nothing ordinary about that. I want your power."

Her cheeks pinked as a scowl marred her forehead.

A current shifted between them. He reached for her, but she stepped away. He wasn't in the mood for games. He wanted her under him. "What troubles you?"

"You." She stepped even farther out of his reach. "What if I can't give you a magical baby? Do you jettison me into space, send me back to the castle, or lock me away so you can pursue this dream of a magical child? I have no way to promise you what you want. And I have no assurance of my place by your side."

"You're mine. I will get what I want, but I also want you. Your magic on my side is enough to keep you safe as long as you always use your power for the good of my empire." He took two steps forward and tucked a loose strand of hair behind her ear. "Does that satisfy your fears? I would not let anyone harm you."

Her expression remained grim, but she gave him a single sharp nod.

He ran his thumb over her lip. "You are fiery. Just remember no matter how big a blaze, it needs air to breathe. Don't make me snuff out that flame inside you. I don't want to break your spirit, but I will if I must."

Her pupils were dilated, and the lids heavy as

she gazed at him. Her breath came out in pants. "And I hope you won't forget a fire can burn you, no matter how small an ember."

He could smell her arousal, and it made her words so much more sensual. He'd been with women of all types, but this was the first time he was intrigued by a female. "You have a beautiful mouth, even when it's being sassy."

She frowned. "Promise me you won't tell me pretty lies. I want your honesty."

He hated how little she thought of herself. She was his, and she was going to accept her value. "Take off her your clothing," he ordered.

She kicked off her thin leather slippers, paused, and looked at him as if for reassurance. He gave her a single firm nod. Her delicate fingers went to the buttons on the front of her dress. He watched in silence as she unbuttoned the front, and her breasts spilled free. She wore no undergarment to restrain her feminine curves. She paused for just a moment and then continued until her dress slipped down over her shoulders to pool around her ankles. She stood bare and perfect.

"Excellent," he uttered, lost to say more.

Her cheeks stained a bright pink as she remained under his watch, vulnerable and nude for his pleasure. And he was very pleased. If he could have painted, she'd have inspired a masterpiece. He'd never seen anything like her.

Sitting on the edge of the bed, he reached out and took her hand. "Lie on my bed -- our bed. You will be my wife in all ways. We will share a life. I don't want cold necessity between us."

Her beautiful face wore a serious expression, but she nodded. He was relieved she didn't protest. Each movement was stiff and guarded as she lay down on the bed. He was still wearing his black flight suit. He chuckled when he noticed she pressed her knees together tight, but then he saw her subtle quaking. He had all the power in her mind, but she had no idea how much control she had over him.

He touched her cheek lightly, and she turned her face into his caress. In that moment, he saw the future they could have together, and it humbled him. If he tamed her, she would be his forever. He would not break her, but instead teach her to bend.

Even without the benefit of time for a slow courtly seduction, he had to be careful with her. If he betrayed her needs selfishly he'd lose this tenuous willingness he glimpsed. He could smell her desire, but that didn't mean she understood what her body craved. Bracing one leg against the bed, he turned, hiding his erection from her as well as he could. He touched her arm, she flinched. But he continued with non-sexual, relaxing strokes against her skin, until he saw a visible change in her posture. He needed her to relax more than this, but it was a start.

The thatch of curls at the junction of her thighs teased him with memories. He was the only one who'd ever been inside her. That stamp of ownership filled his soul. He drew her legs apart, hooking her knees with his hands, and she let him. The first night had been different. She'd been playing a role. Today she was Brisa. His Brisa. And no one else.

She looked away. His fingers brushed her femininity, and her breath caught. Her beautiful submission was a gift. Even tense she let him direct her. He spread her legs wider, and she looked down at her nudity with innocent curiosity. "It was dark."

Her voice broke the spell he was under, and he

had to shake his head to clear his thoughts. "What?"

"When -- when we did this before it was dark. I -- It's so strange."

"You're beautiful. I promised you the truth, and you have it. I like looking at you."

Her frown betrayed her negative thoughts, but he let that go. A lifetime of self-doubt could not be erased with a single truth. Her frown marred her beauty, so he gave her a little physical space. He'd been bred to lead the universe, and a good master of his domain understands said dominion.

He could still see her clearly, but that small bit of room relaxed her more, and he couldn't stop his sly grin. She glanced at his face, her expression a mixture of confusion and shame. He'd teach her to only feel pride and joy in his bed, but like all lessons, this had to start at the beginning. "I know you were innocent before, but did you ever touch yourself to feel pleasure?"

"No. The goddess would have disapproved."

The way she couldn't meet his eyes told him so much more than her lie. "Wife, we are not at the temple. I want to learn what you like. Touch yourself."

She bit her lip, then her tongue darted out to wet her mouth. He wanted to crush her against him and kiss and fuck until spent, but he resisted.

Slowly, her hand slid over her firm pale belly, over the dark hair at the apex of her pussy, and between her tender folds. He said nothing as she rubbed with a single fingertip. He spread her wider, and she moaned. He wanted to taste her, but now was not the time. Teaching her to submit to his wants was killing him, but he knew he had to endure a little pain now for the bounty of her obedience later.

The dew sparkled in the dim light as he watched.

Brisa added another finger as her gentle circles moved faster. She pressed her clit harder. His mouth went dry. Her movements grew serious as her motion became more practiced and natural. A tiny mewling whimper sighed from her lips as her eyes fluttered closed. Her hair twisted, rolled, and tangled on the pillow as she thrashed with the building excitement.

Ka'Sen breathed in the scent of her enjoyment, sighing, as he enjoyed the beauty of her flushed face and her fingers parting her wider, exposing more of her to his view.

"I -- I wish... don't stare so much," she gasped out, and then her hips bucked. A low moan and tiny panting gasp made her embarrassment more charming.

"How will I learn what makes you purr if I don't see you pet that lovely pussy?"

She made a sound that was half shock and half pleasure deep in her throat, but still didn't look at him. Her thrashing intensified. The slickness on her fingers announced she was ready for more as did the twitch of her hips and her needy little cries.

Brisa's toes curled, and her leg jerked. She whimpered, the sound of a woman on the verge of orgasm.

Reaching out, he grabbed her wrists and pulled her hands away. Her eyes opened, and her lips pursed as confusion replaced desire on her expressive face. She tried to reach her clit again, but he held her firm. "From this moment forward" -- he kept his tone gentle, albeit firm --"You will not touch yourself unless I ask you to."

Her breasts rose and fell fast as her shallow breaths huffed out with irritation. He let her go. Her fingers hovered near her clit, but she did not touch herself. He saw her desperation, and for a moment his resolve to teach the lesson wavered. Taking a moment to compose himself and modulate his tone, he took another breath of the heady scent of her desire. His hand found the wet heat between her legs. He watched her face as he strummed the nub between her legs. When he noticed her nibble her lip and close her eyes, he rubbed the spot he'd found, harder.

Her small breasts jiggled as she squirmed under his strokes. Her arousal was so lovely he enjoyed denying her completion.

"Yes. Yes." Her whimpers promised she was at the brink. He took his hand away. Tears leaked from the corners of her eyes. "Why are you doing this to me?"

He stood and began unsnapping the fasteners on his flight suit. The bulky armor took time to remove, and he never stopped watching her torment as he methodically stripped away his clothing layer after layer. "Because there is much more for me to do to you than give you a single orgasm. When you come you will remember the moment for longer than a fleeting flash of biological relief. Your whole body will come for me."

She blinked up at him with a dubious expression. He cocked an eyebrow at her unwitting challenge, grinning as her gaze roamed to his erection. She was right; the last time it had been dark. He could see her looking at his nudity with new eyes. He was well-built. He'd never had a moment of doubt about his body, but with her looking at him with innocent curiosity his buttocks clenched, and he gritted his teeth against a moment of vulnerability he hadn't anticipated.

"Tell me the rule about touching yourself," he demanded.

"Rules? I…"

He was sure his scowl silenced her. "Tell me, and I will give you what you need."

"I won't -- umm -- I won't touch myself unless you ask me to."

He smiled. She pleased him far more than she could know. The next time he'd feast between her legs, but today he wanted her to come only from him inside her. He wanted her to crave his cock.

He moved to the foot of the bed, knelt, and took her ankles in his hands. With a sharp tug he had her close enough to penetrate, but he wanted her to feel him deeper than she would on her back.

"Command, mirror," he said. Her confusion morphed into awe as the aquatic image changed, and the wall became mirrored.

He put his hands on her knees, spreading her legs and rubbed her wetness, letting one of his fingers slide inside her. "I want to be here, deep inside you, but not like before."

She was putty in his hands as he turned her onto her stomach and then pulled her half off the bed until her feet were firmly on the floor. He pressed between her shoulder blades, keeping her bent over, and she stood submissively as he used his knee to widen her legs for easier access.

* * *

Brisa hated herself for wanting this brute so much. She'd never been so turned on in her life, so she yielded to her new husband's whims. She'd learned to submit to survive, but this time she was giving him all that she was out of a need she'd never recognized before. His cock pressed into her ready pussy, stretching her with a satisfying burning that made her push up on her tiptoes and arch into him. He thrust forward, and she whimpered. She rocked back against him, her ass slapped by his muscular body. Each powerful plunge rocked her forward as he went deeper and harder. It felt good, so good.

"Look, sweet witch, look at the mirror. You can't come until you understand," he moaned.

Brisa's brow furrowed as she tried to make sense of his words through the haze of want. "What?" Everything was so out of control. Her pussy ached, and she felt her hot dew run down her thigh as he pulled out. "I'm so close. Please. Please."

"I know," he cooed in a tone as if he were comforting an injured wild creature. "You must accept what we're meant to be. Brisa, look at yourself in the mirror. See what I see."

He nudged the tip of his thick erection inside her again. She bucked against him, slapping her ass against him and taking him as deep as she could. Grinding against him, she put her forehead against the mattress, groaning in frustration.

Ka'Sen took her chin in his hand and gently lifted her head. "Look."

She blinked open her eyes to see. His strong, powerful body, inserted inside her. Her hair was tousled. Her high cheekbones were painted scarlet, and her eyes were heavy-lidded. Her lips were swollen. Everything about them screamed sensuality -- not just sex. She appeared ethereal. She'd only meant to take a quick look to satisfy him, but now she saw his vision.

"You're beautiful. You're the princess of every known world under my authority. See who you are. Tell me!"

"I'm… I'm yours. Please. I can't stand it. Please," she honestly sobbed. "I'm whatever you want me to be."

And there it was. She understood why he tormented her now. She accepted his plan for her and his demands as she lay strung out and sobbing against his bed. She'd break into a million pieces if he didn't give her more.

"Your pretty pussy was made just for me, sweet witch." His voice was rough and strained. "You take all of me so well." He groaned low in his throat. "So tight."

Lust stole her breath from her lungs. "Please!"

Closing her eyes against the shame, she tried to deny how much she didn't want him to stop. She sacrificed her dignity for pleasure, concentrating on the sensation, wailing with pleasure as she hovered on the brink of ecstasy.

His hand caressed her back and neck, making every nerve ending come alive as he fucked her with a ferocity that stole her breath. Eager to the point of mortification, Brisa arched into his touch and responded with primal grunts to his every pet and stroke, completely his in the moment. She screamed as the first wave of release crashed into her and sent her spiraling blindly into orgasm. Tears leaked from the corners of her eyes as her soul caught fire, and everything became liquid with the rolling bliss of each new blast of pleasure as her senses heightened.

Ka'Sen pressed his hand firmly against her pubic bone, and she gasped as he felt even bigger. When his long index finger stroked her clit, she shook. Her pussy clenched around him, and her mind clouded in a fog of pleasure. Her whole being focused on the amazing feeling as she came harder than she'd ever come in her life.

"So good," Ka'Sen growled. "Brisa! By the gods!"

She squealed with the crescendo of her climax, and the heat of his release spilled into her throbbing pussy. Her inner muscles continued to spasm around him as he managed to get them both on the bed with his cock still deep inside her.

For a long, quiet moment, he held her. Sweat cooled her as it dried, and she shivered.

"Cover us," Ka'Sen ordered, and the blanket pulled up from the bottom of the bed to slither over their nakedness. She was too spent to marvel at the enchanted bed. Her pussy still throbbed, driving his seed deeper. Her eyes fluttered closed, and she yawned.

Her prince had commanded her to give him a powerful baby to rule the stars, and after that performance she had little doubt he'd get what he wanted. Exhaustion from the traumatic events coupled with his mastery of her drove Brisa into a deep, dreamless sleep.

Chapter Four

Brisa paced the room. Wrapped in the bedsheet she felt too off-balance. She'd woken, alone, in Ka'Sen's -- their -- room. Her dress and shoes were gone. A more feminine version of Reven's uniform was draped over the long bench. There was a pair of the strange, shiny black boots the men wore, as well.

Everything looked the right size to fit her, but she'd never donned anything like these clothes. Pants were not for decent ladies. She might have acted like a whore in his bed, but she was still a lady. She wanted her dress. That one piece of who she was would make all the difference when she felt so out-of-control.

The mirror was gone, replaced by a beautiful garden. Birds flew from tree to tree, and there was a tranquil pond shimmering. Leaves dropped into the water, sending ripples over the surface. If she hadn't been so upset, she'd have enjoyed relaxing to the scene.

The door opened, and Ka'Sen stepped in. Her delight at seeing him mingled with her anger he'd let her wake alone.

"I was alerted you were awake and came as soon as my meeting with my commanders ended. They've extended heartfelt congratulation to us both." He paused, and his head tilted a little to the side. "Why aren't you dressed?"

"Because my dress is missing."

He shook his head. "First we get you clean. Come."

She followed him to a closet.

"Step inside."

She wasn't a fan of tight spaces. "Are you kidding?"

"I think you know I don't."

He was right, no sense of humor. "Why?"

"Cleansing. Trust me."

Reluctantly, she stepped into the tight space.

"Hold still," he cautioned. "Sanitize," he said a little louder.

A foul-smelling mist hit her, and she screamed. The awful stuff got in her mouth, and she coughed and choked it out. When it ended a moment later her skin dried almost immediately, and she did feel fresh, but Ka'Sen's grin angered her. "Did you know it was going to do that?"

"Of course. Don't worry, the stuff is harmless. At least your breath will be as clean as the rest of you."

"Gee, thanks."

"Come. Let's get you dressed."

"Where are my things?"

"I had them incinerated."

"You *what*?"

"My bride won't wear those primitive things. You'll wear the proper uniform."

"So, I'm part of the crew now?"

"Of course not, too many years of training involved with that. No, you're my wife. My warrior princess, if you like."

She did not, but she held her tongue.

After a small amount of coaxing, she wore the uniform he called a flight suit. It fit her far too closely, making her feel naked even under several layers because the fabric was so formfitting. "You really want me to leave the room dressed like this?"

He nodded. "You are perfect. Don't make me show you again."

Heat warmed her cheeks as a memory of last night's mirrored scene. "We wouldn't want that."

He grinned. "Are you sure?"

She wasn't, but she was curious enough about the ship to step out into the hall dressed as he'd requested.

"Let's get you some food. You'll need to replenish after all that exercise."

Her face heated as a formation of soldiers passed, paying them no more attention than to extend a quick bow toward the prince. Another group, dressed all in very plain white uniforms, marched past in the other direction. They also bowed curtly in unison. Everyone seemed to be in a hurry.

"Is something happening?"

"Something is always happening. Why?"

"Everyone is rushing by so fast. At home if you don't stop to exchange some sort of pleasantry you'd be considered rude."

"Things here move at a different pace. As I said, there are many vids I want you to see to gain an understanding of the wider universe. I will keep you close until you've had a chance to learn a bit more. If anyone mocks you, I will have them put to death."

Her heart gave a pained leap. "Dear goddess, no!" She hoped he was exaggerating. Life was far too precious for such a casual execution order. "Promise me you will never kill on my account."

"Brisa --"

"Promise me this, please."

Something flickered in his eyes, and he gave her a single nod. "You are my wife. Don't forget your position and none will die for you."

She didn't fully comprehend his meaning, but the ominous statement hung between them as Ka'Sen led her through corridor after corridor. No color populated his world. Just neutral tones and black.

Depressing. She missed nature already. "How do I… I… prevent you from killing?"

He gave her an offended side-eyed glance. "You take a lot of responsibility for what happens to those around you. The only thing I want you to focus on is magic."

"I've been hiding my magic for so long I'm not sure what good it will do you."

He grunted. "Come up with something small, but impressive. When I introduce you today, I want you to show my people that I have your power on my side."

"You saw me create a gift, not exactly something to inspire awe." She looked away.

"That small act has kept me under your spell."

Her gaze jerked up to meet his. Heat warmed her face. "I don't want to do this. I'm not made of the same material as you or the real princess. I'm just a girl."

"And that is all the more reason I need you at my side. I want my legacy to be more than fear." His eyes sparkled with a wild light as he stopped short. She gasped as he gripped her shoulders and pulled her to face him. "Help me build a better universe."

He was asking a lot. A lot. She bit her lip. "How?"

"We start with breakfast."

Her appetite was gone, but she went with him. A few curious stares were quickly ended when Ka'Sen noticed. Fear radiated from these people. She saw people who'd just sat down with food get up and scurry out when they entered. She wanted to ask him what he'd done to make his own warriors fear him but decided on prudent silence.

The room was brightly lit. Various platters and plates sat ready in glass cases. She saw a brightly colored glob taken by a bald female with red eyes. Most of the people on the ship looked like her and Ka'Sen, but every now and again she noticed someone unusual. She knew he'd said there were other planets, but she didn't understand why the people looked different if they'd all originated from her world. She filed away the question for later and tried not to stare. "What's this?" She opened the door and took out what looked like a colorful mixture of plants.

"You'll like that. It's a favorite of people from more natural planets, like yours. It's been created with a balance of vitamins and protein to give you optimal nutrition."

She frowned. "Sounds delicious."

"Here." He handed her a small package. "Give it a try."

She took the item and followed him to a table. When she sat, he put his plate down next to hers, then left, only to return with two steaming cups. He set one next to her. She watched him take a drink before she tried the liquid. It was hot and sweet. She liked the little perk it gave her. She took another sip before she noticed him watching her.

Ka'Sen grinned. They ate in silence. She forced herself to consume the food. He had expectations, and she'd need energy to try and meet them. "When do you need me to prove I have magic?"

A loud bell chimed. "All non-essential personnel to the flight deck. Repeat. All non-essential personnel to the flight deck." He took a drink and set his empty mug down. "As soon as you're finished eating."

Her meal congealed into a lump in her stomach. "You don't mess around, do you? I -- a little time would have been nice."

"Every day this rebellion stirs, people die. Time

is not a luxury they have."

He had a good point. She didn't understand anything about his world, but if doing a little something for show would save even one life she was happy to come up with a tiny spell. "I don't know if I can even do anything away from the temple. All magic comes from the goddess."

His nostrils flared. She could see him considering her statement. "Why didn't you tell me this before?"

"It's not as if you sat down and asked me for any details about magic. I don't understand it completely myself." She held her hand out and imagined a tiny star. A glow emanated over her palm until a small light shone. "Well, looks like I still have my abilities."

His relief was palpable. "Excellent. Finished?"

She nodded.

"Let's go."

Brisa stood with him. She saw a metallic creature come for their leavings. The oddities here were a never-ending source of questions, but she put that one away with the others in her head and followed Ka'Sen out.

* * *

Ka'Sen watched the faces of the crew in the first few rows. The largest space on Vulture was full. An image of Brisa filled the whole wall behind them so even the farthest back could see the glowing ball in her hands. He could see fear and awe in the faces watching. What he hadn't told Brisa was this being broadcast to each planet under his dominion.

"As you can see my wife has magic. All the greatest weaponry and power in the universe is under my dominion. I know there have been uprisings, but those rebels are being sought and executed. Treachery is doomed. Accept the world I give you or die. There is no other option."

Brisa kept the orb growing as he spoke. Resounding applause followed his words. Now he'd need to see his father's reaction. He'd purposefully kept his plans to himself until it was too late for the elderly ruler to do anything less than support him.

He signaled to cut the transmission, then led Brisa away from the crowd to where Reven stood. "Watch over her. Take her to my room and play her the vids we discussed. You know what I have to do."

His friend's concern was poorly disguised. Reven nodded and took Brisa's elbow. "I will help you find your way back to your room."

Ka'Sen watched them go. Everything was falling into place. She'd done well. He was pleased.

* * *

Hestron and Kello stood watching the girl leave with the prince's bodyguard.

"She doesn't look like much," Hestron whispered. "That little trick was nothing."

"Don't matter what we think of her." Kello ran his hand through his thinning hair. "He thinks she's special. He cares about her. We need her to care about what's happening. The girl has no clue about the monster, but she will."

Hestron nodded. "This could be our only chance to get her to the empress."

They followed the slowly shuffling crowd as people moved forward to return to the posts awaiting them. If the men weren't successful they were dead, and the entire mission would fail. Next time, there would be much more security around the woman. Reven took her to the elevator. They stayed back as the doors closed. The hall emptied. Kello opened the panel and rewired it while Hestron punched in an emergency code and overrode the alarm system.

A moment later, the doors opened, and Reven stood with the woman behind him. He raised his weapon, but Hestron waved his hand in the air, the gun jerked out of the guard's hand.

Reven blanched. "How?"

"Tell Prince Ka'Sen his mother sends her regards." Kello shook his hand in the air and then pinched his fingers together. Reven collapsed on the elevator floor.

The girl shook. Kello held out his hand in offering. "Come. Let us save you."

"Who are you?"

"We are the keepers. We've been protecting magic since the exodus. Come if you want to know the truth behind your power."

She glanced down at Reven, then back at them. Her distrust was not concealed.

"He is fine. We don't have much time." Hestron grabbed her arm, and she struggled.

Kello touched her forehead. "Sleep."

Hestron caught the girl before she hit the ground. Now all they had to do was escape the most powerful man in the galaxy. With will and power they materialized in a transport. It took only a small expenditure of power to make the controllers open the launch doors. And then -- they were free.

* * *

Ka'Sen stood next to his father's bed.

The old king coughed, hard, and his whole body shook. When the ruler recovered, he wiped his mouth on a linen cloth and glared at his son. "Your little announcement was very surprising. What makes you think this girl is any different than your mother? Why would she give you her power? Love?"

"No. Fear. I learned many things at your side, Father, but never about love. I do know fear. She knows nothing of the world, except what I will teach her. She's not our enemy. If we're careful she'll be the greatest treasure in my kingdom, and our children will have the power to bring peace."

"Peace! You and your foolish dreams! I hope this doesn't escalate out of your control. I didn't spend my entire life building something for you to destroy."

"You didn't build this. Our ancestors did."

"No? Think about how unstable things were when you were a boy. Now there are a few foolish terrorists who believe in separatist politics and that the planets should self-govern, but for the most part the worlds are calm. People have prosperity. We've given them a gift by forcing the unification. Our values belong to the masses. Our ways are the only ways. Who are you to disparage my legacy? I built this world for you to inherit. You should have consulted me."

"It's done. She's mine, and nothing you say will change that. The people -- all the people have seen her. They've seen her power."

"You don't know anything about power."

"And whose fault is that? You killed everyone with magic before I was born, sparing only my mother."

"And a poorer choice I could not have made. I just don't want you to repeat my mistakes. Magic users aren't like the rest of us. Now you've brought one from the sacred home world."

"Exactly. She's a blank slate. She will live for our cause. She will live for me."

The king opened his mouth to reply, but a knock on the door interrupted him. "Enter."

Reven rushed inside. "Ka, we have a problem."

"Can this wait?" Ka'Sen asked. He really felt he'd made progress convincing his father of the wisdom in his plan.

"No. You both need to see this." Reven pulled up a vid on the wall.

Horrified, Ka'Sen watched his bride taken by two traitors. She'd resisted. His terror wasn't for his legacy, it was for his woman. "Where are they?"

"Escaped." Reven rubbed the back of his neck. "There's more."

Ka'Sen didn't want to consider how this could get worse.

Reven took a deep breath and let it out slowly. "She's pregnant. All the health scans taken while she slept are back. She has some malnutrition, but otherwise she's healthy. The conception took place the night of your marriage. Congratulations."

Feelings Ka'Sen had never endured before swirled through him. Protective urges roared to life making his panic worse. The traitors who had his wife also held the life of his unborn in their hands. The thought he might never see his child sent a shaft of pain through his heart. Would the child have her kind eyes? When he got them back he was never letting them leave the room without him again. He'd been a fool to believe she was safe.

His father wore a look of satisfaction. "If you'd only come to me we'd have made sure your plan was successful. I am not a well man, but I will live to see your child. We will get your woman back. *Grandfather.* I never thought I'd live to see you continue our line. If we get her back quickly enough we might be able to salvage your plan. If these men are cruel to her it will only help convince her of our cause over theirs."

Ka'Sen didn't like the way his father was using Brisa's suffering to their advantage. She hadn't gone willingly. The idea gave him comfort, but then the memory of the fear on her face sent rage burning through his veins. "How long ago?"

"Not long. During the last rotation. Problem is they were smart enough to disable the tracking on the craft they stole. I'm sorry. I failed you."

"We will get her back," Ka'Sen said emphatically. "She will be safe with me again soon."

* * *

"She's waking."

Brisa stirred, then froze. The memory of her kidnapping was the first thing to come to mind.

"No use pretending," said a female voice. "You're safe, girl."

Brisa opened her eyes. An older woman sat next to her. She was tall and pale. Her dark hair had a streak of gray running through it, but she'd piled the thick locks in an elaborate style on top of her head. The woman's face was strangely familiar, but Brisa couldn't place the stranger. "Where am I?"

"You're free, and safe. How are you feeling?" The woman held out a mug of fragrant liquid.

Birsa accepted the offering. "My head hurts." She eyed the cool liquid dubiously.

"This will make you feel better. A sleep spell is unnatural and always leaves the head aching. This will help. We wouldn't bring you all this way to poison you."

She took a small sip. It wouldn't make sense to bring her here and kill her. The stuff was sweet. She took a bigger drink. Her dry mouth felt better and so did her head. "Thanks." Looking around she saw they were in a small cabin. The walls were covered with cooking implements and other practicalities of farming. They couldn't be in space anymore. "Where am I?"

"I guess you'll find out soon enough. This is Amidora. My name is Mai'Sen."

"Do I know you? You seem so familiar."

The woman gave her a sad smile. "You know my son."

"Who's your son?"

"Trust your intuition. Who do you think?"

Brisa gasped. "Ka'Sen?"

Mai'Sen nodded. "Our spies said he sought magic. When I learned he was going to the sacred home world I assumed he was planning to take a bride. I'm sorry I'm right. It's not safe to take you back there, but I promise we'll hide you."

"Why would you betray him if you're his mother?"

Her sad eyes brightened with unshed tears. "I haven't seen him since he was a very young boy. His father is twisted and evil. The things my son has done in his father's name shame me. I'm sorry for your suffering."

How could Brisa explain to this woman that she wanted to return to Ka'Sen? She didn't even understand why. "Your son is not a bad man."

Mai'Sen's eyes widened. "You were with him willingly?"

"No -- not at first. I -- He's not a bad man. He needs someone to help him find peace."

"I thought that about his father too, but power corrupts."

They remained silent for a time. Finally, Brisa sighed. "I need to go back."

"Why? We went through a lot of trouble to get you away from there."

"I didn't ask you to do that. There are children on the ship who need me."

"Children? Are they my son's?" Mai'Sen sounded terrified.

"No."

"Yours?"

"In a sense. They are orphans in my care. They'll be frightened if I don't return."

"I'm sorry. We didn't know about them. It's too late to get them out now, but for their sakes you can't go back."

"I must."

"There's too much at stake." Mai'Sen took her hand. "See."

Brisa's eyes fluttered closed.

* * *

Fires burned everywhere. The smell of smoke and burning flesh stung her nostrils. Brisa's eyes burned as she tried to see what was coming through the flames. Embers floated around her, stinging her arms and singeing her hair. She wanted to scream, but no sound came. Ka'Sen stepped out of the carnage. Blood ran in rivers from the bodies scattered all over the ground. She recognized this place, but knew she'd never actually been there. She realized this spot had future significance and the memories of the location hadn't been made yet which left her off balance in a surreal haze of confusion. He looked so angry.

She wanted to call out to him, help him, but she couldn't move or speak. He walked past without seeing her. She watched him cut down unarmed men and women. A child fell under his blade. She ached with each death. Her soul screamed, but her silent watch was pure punishment. And then, he turned, looking right at her. "Why?"

She didn't know what he was asking her, and her silent voyeurism didn't allow her to question him. She held out her arms.

"We could have ruled the world. Why did you betray me?"

She hadn't. How could she declare her innocence when she couldn't speak?

He turned, cutting down more terrified people. She wanted to beg him to stop, but all she could do was watch.

* * *

Brisa's eyes opened. She was back. "What was that?"

"The future."

"There's no such thing. The future isn't a promise, it's a hope. I can fix this. He -- he thought I betrayed him."

"You spoke to him?" Mai'Sen's eyes widened.

"Not exactly, but he saw me. He wanted to know why I had betrayed him. But I haven't. There's still hope that the future you showed me is a lie."

"The only lie is that he can be saved."

"You're his mother. How can you give up on him?"

Mai'Sen's gaze narrowed. "You haven't met his father, have you?"

"No, but we aren't our parents. We are a collection of our own choices."

"My son's fate was set the moment he was forced on me."

The bitterness in the woman's tone told Brisa something terrible had transpired to make her so angry, but that still didn't make her son guilty.

Mai'Sen gave her a sad smile. "Your loyalty is commendable. I'm glad my son has not hurt you, but he will hurt others. He has hurt innocents."

"He isn't all bad. There's hope."

The older woman shook her head. "Hope is a luxury of youth. The time for me to fix past mistakes is long over. I have to end this. I have to fix what happened because I couldn't end my infant's life."

Brisa gasped. "Dear goddess, what a terrible thing to consider. He was a helpless babe. There is good in him. If you can blame his father for the bad, can you at least claim the good in him. Help me save him."

The indecision on the woman's face was stark in contrast to her earlier resolve. "I wish I could see what you do. He's lost."

"No. There's still hope!"

Mai'Sen's eyes misted. "Yes. Only one. I hope we can end his life before my vision comes to pass."

Brisa's heart ached.

The older woman touched Brisa's forehead. "Sleep."

She could have sworn she heard Ka'Sen say her name as she lost consciousness.

Command His Heart (Commanded 3)

Ashlynn Monroe

At the mercy of her kidnappers -- and her new mother-in-law -- Brisa wants to find her place in the universe. While she worries about the fate of her littles, the orphans she left behind when she was kidnapped by rebels, she also realizes she needs to start worrying about herself if she's ever going to be able to help anyone else. She's been a pawn her whole life, but this is her chance to choose her path. Freedom? Or return to Ka'Sen's side? She senses there is more to her husband than simply following in his brutal father's footsteps. Even if his own mother can't see his potential for goodness, Brisa does. Can she free the man who seeks to imprison her?

Ka'Sen believed his mother was dead, but now she has resurfaced as the leader of *The Great Eyes*, the rebels who seek to end his legacy. Worse, his resurrected mother has taken his wife from him. News that should have brought him joy heightens the stakes, and this revelation leaves him unsure of himself for the first time in a very long time. Is he willing to see the wonder of the universe through his wife's eyes, or will he let power blind him to the potential of a future that hasn't been written yet?

Brisa must decide between love and doing what's right. When the only happiness you've ever had is slipping from reach, how do you find the courage to save worlds?

Chapter One

Freedom.

Brisa ran through the field overlooking her home. The castle where she'd been raised as a foundling lay majestically in the valley below. The land around the estate was the bright emerald of springtime. Strangely, when she looked down there was no fear, nor the usual apprehension that went with being out in the open, and away from her many chores. She made it to the tree line of the forest.

She couldn't remember why she'd been given this precious free time, but the pure exuberance filled her with rare happiness. Sun shone through the leaves. She could smell the fresh air. And then thunder rumbled to the north. Turning, Brisa saw the darkness approaching, and she could sense the rolling storm begin in the distance, heading for her, brutal.

Her whole body shook and disorientation set in. Her sleep-addled mind clung to the remnants of the dream. A moment later, she blinked open her eyes into the darkness of an unfamiliar place as low murmurs filtered softly into her dreams. The industrial smells of the craft reminded her she was a long way from home. She'd awoken in the stars. And she wasn't alone.

She shut her eyes again and held still.

Listening hard, she could make out the voice of Mai'Sen, a woman claiming to be the mother of her husband -- a husband she wasn't sure she wanted. If he didn't hold the fate of two children she loved in his hands, she would slip away and find a nook in the vast universe where she could live in peace and safety. Uncomplicated.

Fighting to keep her breathing even, she

pretended to sleep.

A soft throat clearing was far louder than it should have been in the silent room. Brisa froze, unwilling to give up her ruse.

"I know you're awake," said Mai'Sen. "We've arrived."

A beat of panic made Brisa's breath catch. Without knowing the destination, she couldn't muster any relief.

"There's no use pretending." Mai'Sen didn't hide her irritation. "Rise up and help me. The universe needs you."

It was Brisa's turn to be upset. Her eyes opened as she sat up to glare at the older woman. "What has the universe ever done for me?"

A sad smile tilted Mai'Sen's mauve lips up in a quick twitch. There was a similarity to Ka'Sen around the woman's eyes and mouth. Her dark hair and darker eyes had been passed down to her handsome son. "You're not asking the right question."

Brisa glared. "No?"

"No. What does the universe hold in store for you? A future. Freedom. These are the things I want you to think about. Don't look behind you. Look ahead."

Brisa glanced away. She fought to hide the churning emotion bubbling from a deep well of long-ignored sorrow. All she'd ever dreamed of was a simple life of her own choosing. She was as far from home as she'd ever been, and still she was bound to the whims of others. "How will I find my liberation when I'm always following someone else's command? I just want to find a quiet place where I can be at peace."

"Imagine you find this spot." Mai'Sen raised her arm with a flourish. "You have a little cottage, a garden, maybe a child or two. You aren't reliant on anyone but the planet. You breathe free air and drink free water. Life rolls on in an endless stream of common existence. Then one day you wake up and there are craft hovering about. Your children are terrified. Your whole world is under siege. A great battle lays waste to your garden and cottage. You found peace, but did you hold it?"

"You're trying to scare me."

Mai'Sen's eyes darkened. "You should be scared. The example I gave you has happened countess times. I've seen the end of everything. I birthed the Great Destroyer."

Brisa's breath caught in her throat. She'd heard the priestess whispering with her accolades about the prophecy. "The Great Destroyer? Do you worship the goddess?"

Mai'Sen flinched. "Long ago. Now I worship the Void."

Brisa stood up so fast she tumbled as she tried to back away from the terrorist. Even on her home world she'd heard of the violent deeds of those who were trying to bring about the end of all life everywhere.

"Calm yourself," Mai'Sen ordered.

Trembling, Brisa couldn't ignore her terror. She was under the power of maniacs. Mai'Sen's pseudo religion believed humanity needed to end for the natural world to heal from the scars left by civilization. Brisa's gaze darted around the room, desperate. Mai'Sen's faith was dangerous. Her cult committed genocide and believed they'd be rewarded by reincarnation into a new race of spiritual beings if they brought about the end of all worlds.

Trapped, Brisa stumbled as she tried backing away. There was nowhere to run, but that didn't stop her from trying.

Mai'Sen crossed the small space and grabbed Brisa's arm. "I'm saving you from so much pain. You're the key to stopping this."

The woman was crazy. "What? Stopping what?"

Mai'Sen searched Brisa's face with a wild gaze that was both unnerving and somehow sad at the same time. "I'm preventing you from watching everything you care about die. You have no idea how empty you can be until you have nothing left of your soul. You'll thank me someday soon. If you're frightened now; so be it." Regret colored her tone.

"I don't understand."

"You will," Mai'Sen's voice dropped an ominous octave. "Your *husband* will destroy everything."

Brisa shook off her hold. "Your *son* isn't the one who gave an entire colony the plague."

"We saved them. They were slaves, raping that moon for minerals. Most of them already had lung diseases. They were killing themselves anyway."

"Killing them saved them?"

"Yes. We kept their souls from the purge of spirits."

"I don't want to know anything more about your stupid religion. The goddess would never condone killing. Your beliefs are a bastardization of her teachings."

Mai'Sen paled. "It's be a very long time since I talked to anyone who was a follower of the goddess. Your naiveté is sweet, but doomed. I won't let you play your part in your husband's success."

Curiosity trumped Brisa's fear. "Why do you hate your son?"

"I don't hate him. I hate what his father has made him. There is a vast difference. I pulled you out before you found out what it's like to watch your flesh and blood twist into a monster. He cannot know about his magic."

"What?" Shock clouded her mind momentarily. "He said he needs a child with magic. Are you telling me he *is* a child of magic?" *Like me? Like my sister?* Somehow the idea that he didn't really need her wasn't the relief it should have been.

"I've said too much. Just know I've worked every day since the day he was born to keep him from using magic. You are not going to ruin everything I've done for the last thirty years. He will not have you, or your child."

"I don't have a child. You separated us in time." Brisa's thoughts were still stuck on the fact that Ka'Sen had his own magic. Her sister had tried binding Brisa's magic once, and the effort had put Val'Trea in bed for a week recovering her strength. Mai'Sen had to have incredible power to hold a binding for three decades.

Another sad shadow passed over Mai'Sen's face. "You will. You are only a few days into your pregnancy. Our scanners alerted us the moment you came onboard. I'd say congratulations, but there is nothing happy about a child the Great Destroyer wants as much as he wants this one. I should kill you, but I can't bring myself to do it. Sentiment is a sin I have yet to cleanse from my essence. I was never able to love my son, but if you join us I might be able to love my grandchild."

Air whooshed from Brisa's lungs as if she'd been hit, drawing a gasp from her. Trembling, she made her way back to the bed and sat down. "In truth?"

Mai'Sen nodded. "In truth." This time, her expression was kind when she looked at Brisa. "It's a burden I'd hoped to prevent by taking you, but my son is as virile as his father. I, too, carried a monster's child before my marriage was sealed a full cycle. I know the pain of being forced and the hope for a baby unwanted, but nonetheless loved. I'm sorry."

This was not a conversation Brisa wanted to have with Ka'Sen's mother. Ka'Sen was not a monster. He hadn't hurt her. The worst part was she wanted to see him again. She wanted to tell him she carried his child. "Your son is not as bad as you think."

Mai'Sen's eyes narrowed. "I would hate to have to kill you. Join me. I will give you time to think about your child, but also you deserve to see what kind of being its father would twist it into. This dynasty of evil *must* end. It ends with us. Today."

Before Brisa could protest, Mai'Sen pushed herself into Brisa's mind. Disorientation caused queasiness to swirl in her stomach.

* * *

Sunlight bathed the little house in brightness. Mai'Sen stooped to pick beans off the vine. She already had a nice assortment of root vegetables and soon Kiro would be home with something from the butcher. His work in the mine paid well, but she hated the danger he put himself in.

"Momma!" She turned to see Halla in the doorway. Her sweet blonde baby girl would never replace her lost son, but the little one had gone a long way in healing her heart, as had Kiro, Halla's father. He was the most giving man in the universe. For the first time in her life she was truly happy. She could use her magic here without fear. She could just live.

"Come out and help Momma pick supper."

Halla rushed outside, barefoot, and started picking low on the vine.

The high-pitched whine in the sky was her first indication something out of the ordinary was happening. A warbird, the alliance's space-to-terrestrial fighter, came swooping down low enough to be seen below the clouds. It headed right for the hill where the mine operated. Brisa stood frozen as it fired. Rock exploded out of the hills. The forest around the mountain caught flame. A crater replaced the mine. Her mind struggled to grasp what she'd seen. Kiro and his fellow miners were gone -- dead. The ground shook beneath her hard enough that she fell. She sat in the dirt watching smoke billowing from the hillside. Screaming from the village in the valley echoed, and the smell of minerals burning choked her. Halla wept. She tugged on her mother's arm, but shock left Mai'Sen's gaze fixed on the hill. Kiro was her heartbeat. Could he have survived? Another blast shook the ground again as the warbird returned. Halla screamed, high-pitched and terrified. She ran back into the cottage.

Mai'Sen didn't stop her child. She was too confused to think clearly. Why would the alliance attack them? *Her.* Could Ka'Lor know she was here? Had her brutal husband found her?

More warbirds danced over the village in a grotesque ballet of death. The bright glow of fire and echoed explosions killed something deep and fundamental inside Mai'Sen. Smoke turned late afternoon into twilight. Darkness enveloped her soul to match the sky. The whistle of a warbird directly overhead woke Mai'Sen from her horror enough that the instinct to live kicked on. She pushed herself off the ground. "Halla! Come to Momma!"

Ear splitting, the whistle and vibration from the craft above her increased her disorientation. She ran, stumbling, toward the cottage. The shadow of the warbird loomed over her home. "Halla!"

The explosion threw her backward, but she watched her home, and her child, burn with a heat that charred her soul until she welcomed death. Kneeling, she waited to die, but she kept breathing. She couldn't go on without them.

The sky overhead was a mosaic of smoke as she landed, hard, but alive. She tried to scream for her daughter, but the breath was knocked out of her lungs. The noxious cloud of smoke choked her the moment she gasped in a breath and made her lightheaded. She crawled toward the burning cottage. Her throat ached as she tried to say Halla, but only a croak whistled out of her.

A figure in a long gray cloak stepped out of the billowing murkiness of the smoky path. "There's nothing you can do. Come with me and live to fight the alliance."

His voice held the quiver of old age, but also a steely strength Mai'Sen desperately needed. The cottage was almost burned out now, the fire so hot the metal in the doorframe melted. Charred stone remained, but everything wooden was gone. She could see into the destruction and there was no movement. No sign of her child. This was a fire that consumed bone. And only one man could have ordered this.

She turned away from the husk of her home. "Do you swear you want to end Ka'Lor and his alliance?" In the hazy light she couldn't see the man's face. The sunshine was totally obscured with the unnatural cloud of destruction. Burning embers rained around him with a surreal glow.

"It is all that matters. I wish the destruction of everything."

In that second, whatever was left of Mai'Sen fully embraced the man's philosophy. "As do I." She stood on trembling legs and followed him down the road, leaving her unscathed basket of vegetables behind in the dust of her old existence.

* * *

When Mai'Sen released her, Brisa wiped away the tears rolling down her cheeks. "I'm sorry that happened to you." The pathetic platitude was all she could manage.

"Countless people can tell the same story. Ka'Lor kills without remorse, and Ka'Sen will be an even more brutal ruler. It's prophecy that's coming true. Your child cannot fall under his control. I believe in the destruction, but the Great Destroyer will burn so much that the resurrection will not be possible. Every single molecule of nature will burn with civilization."

Brisa shivered.

* * *

Ka'Sen paced, his gaze riveted on a holovid of his wife. Brisa looked beautiful in the picture he'd captured from the security camera. Her big blue eyes were innocent. She was combing out her long dark hair. This private moment, stolen without her knowledge, was all he had of her now. He couldn't believe she'd been taken from right under his nose. Anger and embarrassment battled for supremacy, but they were well matched.

His rage that Brisa was in danger waned only when he thought about the fact that he'd been able to hang on to his woman but a few days. He was the most powerful man on any inhabited world, yet someone had taken the person he wanted most in the universe from him.

What a joke I have become. Powerless. Imagining his troops snickering at him sent his fist into the wall, denting the metal and crumpling the facade of decorative neutral overlay that hid the bones of his ship.

Bones. His wife was delicate, and easily broken. *What are they doing to you, my Brisa? My love?*

He imagined her hurt or afraid, and fear cycled through him again, sending a chill skittering down his spine. Emotion swilled to a crescendo spiking dark and cold in his soul.

His door comm beeped. "Who is it?" he bellowed. Few would risk approaching him until his wife was returned.

"Reven."

"Enter." Reven was the only man Ka'Sen trusted.

When the door closed behind Rev, Ka'Sen's most trusted friend saluted.

"Be at ease. Do you have news?" Ka' Sen held his breath as hope surfaced.

"I have news. Sit."

That couldn't be good, but Ka'Sen sat in the nearest chair. "The scanner has been tampered with, but our tech team was able to reconstruct the signal. She was taken by three people. We have their bio scans being sent to every enforcer in the alliance, even the bounty hunters."

"Good." It was a start. Rev shifted his weight nervously. "Is there more?"

"Yes." Rev hesitated. "She is pregnant."

The words took a moment to sink in. "Brisa?"

Rev smiled, his look amused, albeit sad. "How many other wives do you have?" His look sobered again. "I'm so sorry. We will find her -- them."

"Them." As Ka'Sen repeated the word, he

wondered if she even knew. When she found out, how would she feel about his child? *His child.* When he had wanted a magical being to manipulate he hadn't realized he'd think about that being as a child, let alone *his* child.

Now the idea that Brisa carried his seed filled him with a surge of protectiveness that made him even more desperate to find her, to hold her. He loved Brisa. At some point he'd fallen completely in love with her. The idea that she'd gifted him with the thing he wanted most made that love even better.

"Ka?" When he glanced up at Rev he saw the concern clearly in the way his brow furrowed and his lips compressed. "We will get her back."

"Yes, we will. Thank you, dear friend, I'm glad you told me."

"Congratulations."

Ka'Sen smiled sadly. "Save that for when we have them both home and safe. If one hair on her head is out of place I will torture those bastards until death is the only thing they want, and then I will only let them have it very slowly. A title and a fortune for her return. We must keep her pregnancy a secret. That doesn't leave this room. Have every tech who saw the message killed if you have any questions about their loyalty."

Rev's eyes widened, but he nodded. He reached out and touched Ka'Sen's shoulder lightly. "The knowledge will be protected. When we get her back, I swear on my life I will not let her or the child fall to harm again."

"I don't blame you for her kidnapping."

"I blame myself."

"As I blame myself, but regret and blame will not help her now."

Rev nodded, and turned to leave, but paused with a concerned glance back. He nodded a final time before the door hissed closed behind him. Ka'Sen sat alone in the dim room with his fears. Everything bright in his world was missing.

Chapter Two

Brisa closed her eyes. Thoughts of Ka'Sen nibbled at her mind as she drifted off to sleep.

* * *

"Bu -- but," Brisa struggled for the right thing to say. She didn't want to offend him. "Husband, I can't. I've already -- twice."

Ka'Sen grinned. "Say it again."

"What?" Her head tilted to the side.

"*Husband.* Say it."

Brisa felt her face heat. There was no reason for her to be shy around this man who had taught her so much about pleasure, about her own body, but he could still make her blush. "And if I refuse?" She couldn't help playing with him. Watching his eyes darken as his expression morphed from playful to powerful was to peer into his soul. She wanted to dance with his dangerous side.

"Remember, you begged for this. The things you promised to do with your hands and your mouth... and yet you would rob me of your sweet whisper?"

Brisa pressed her lips together. He backed away.

She gasped. "Imagining it is... different."

He stepped closer and palmed her pussy. His thumb found her clit, and he rubbed gently. Moaning, she closed her eyes. Memory of her lust-fueled pleading burned in her brain as he inserted his long, thick finger, and she tensed around the digit with a shudder. Her hands remained tied over her head. She never wanted to be free.

Under his weight, the bed dipped. Her eyes drifted open and their gazes met, then dropped to where his cock rested between her thighs.

"Different? I don't see how." He bent to feather kisses on her mound. "Or I can let you go. You can imagine this instead."

Brisa quieted.

He chuckled as she pouted. The way he looked at her warmed her.

"Relax for me, wife." He found the lubricant next, stoppered up in a little jar, and dipped his index finger. She jerked with a quick intake of breath as he followed the cleft of her backside. "I promised to never hurt you, but also I vowed to teach you every pleasure."

Brisa let go of the breath she held as he spread her, inserting one finger, then two, knuckles sliding past each other and stretching the tight ring of her sphincter. She wiggled as the virgin opening burned. She turned her heat-flushed face away from him, the silence lingering until she began breathing normally as he stroked in and out of her. She groaned.

He withdrew his fingers and picked up a plug, then set it down, only to pick up the slightly larger one, applying lubricant until the object dripped. "Next step, love," he whispered, ignoring her jerk of surprise as the cold, hard surface touched her anus and pressed against her opening.

"Wait!" Brisa cried.

"Relax, wife. It's small. Don't panic."

Gritting her teeth, she gulped down a deep breath as he continued applying pressure to the plug. Her eyes remained shut tight. "Is it in?"

"Yes. It went in very easy. We will start conservatively and work our way to more advanced play, love."

"You'd better, husband."

Ka'Sen worked the plug out and back in with slow deliberation. "I should leave you tied to my bed as a punishment. You can suffer your desire until you learn to curb that sassy tongue."

"I... please." Her breath whooshed out. "Oh, that -- feels -- all right."

"Just all right?" He wiggled it, twisting, until she moaned.

He rubbed her clit, hard with his free hand until she cried out, panting. "Good! Feels -- good."

He pulled it out completely and she opened her eyes, only to see he'd moved to an even larger plug, working it gently back and forth until most of it stayed inside her. She whimpered, a small mix of pleasure and pain.

"How does it feel?"

"Too big," she mumbled. "But --"

"Yes?"

"Good. I want to try more."

He grinned, and she moaned as he worked the plug deeper inside her.

The ropes held her, even as she thrashed. Her desire climbed higher. "Please." Her gaze found his. "Please, *please* --"

He yanked his leather pants down, pulling his cock free, groaning as he tugged at the base to hold off his own orgasm. "Please what?"

"I want --" Brisa's gaze fixed on his cock. She licked her dry lips. "I want to come."

"Not yet..."

* * *

Brisa awoke aching and grumpy -- and alone. Her arousal burned. Dreams of being with Ka'Sen left her homesick for her husband. She should be happy, seeing Mai'Sen as a savior, not a captor, but she didn't. After enduring Mai'Sen's memory she realized she didn't want to hide away in some obscure corner of the universe. She had the chance to save Ka'Sen. And he was worth saving. Neither of them had known loving parents, but maybe the life inside her could experience the adoration of family.

Family. Her throat tightened.

Wetness on her cheeks caused her to open her eyes. She hadn't even realized she was crying. Her powerful husband could make the world beautiful. She had the chance to influence him to feel empathy for the countless people he ruled. Wiping away the moisture, she felt a strange peace as certainty filled her. Mai'Sen might not believe in her son, but Brisa did. She just had to figure out how to get back to him.

The craft had landed some time ago, but they'd left Brisa in the cargo hold. She shivered. The temperature had slowly begun dropping ever since they'd hit the turbulence of atmosphere. Her breath froze each time she exhaled. She pulled a tarp around her shoulders. Her clothing was not meant for extreme temperatures. She wished she had one of the flight suits made of adaptable fabric. She'd be perfectly comfortable instead of freezing if she had even the lowliest soldier's clothing on instead of the clothing her husband had chosen to display her in the day she was kidnapped.

When the door opened, Brisa jumped. Mai'Sen entered along with two big burly men. "I did not mean to leave you here so long, but we had to make sure all was secure. The game we play will only have one winner."

Brisa didn't understand, but this didn't feel playful to her. "I'm cold."

Mai'Sen gave her a small nod. "And soon you will be warm. Take her."

Brisa struggled instinctively as the big men each grabbed an arm. No one spoke as they hustled her out of the cargo hold, down the corridor and to the airlock. Her teeth chattered as cold slithered through her, making her muscles ache. "Please. I-I..." She bit her tongue as uncontrollable shaking took hold. "I-I'm so c-cold!" Another subzero blast hit her as they walked through a strange connector. She realized they were boarding another craft. Her legs gave her trouble. This was the most intense cold she'd ever experienced, and mortal fear made her heart leap with painful discordance.

Then they boarded the other craft, and the cold was gone. Breath whooshed from Brisa, but she still shivered.

Mai'Sen pressed a wall comm. "We need a warmer and a small flight suit. Now."

A blur of motion caught Brisa's eye. Next to Mai'Sen a tiny person stood holding a pile of fabric. Horror brought a gasp to her lips as she stared. Its furry cat face and startling green eyes peered up at her, curious. This thing reminded her of the castle's mouse-catching cats. The cook had a fondness for orange kitties and always kept those out of the litters born in the kitchen.

Even in her shock, seeing the unnaturally intelligent feline face made her homesick. Brisa gazed at this strange creature as her mind struggled to make sense of what she was seeing. Where had they brought her? For the first time she realized how little her sheltered world had prepared her for the rest of the universe.

The cat offered Brisa the fabric it held, and she

took the bundle, feeling slightly sick as the furry hand brushed hers. As if sensing her discomfort, the being streaked away in a blur of ginger fluff. She'd never seen anything move like the cat had, and the unexpected speed only intensified her unease.

"Put the warmer over your shoulders." Mai'Sen ordered. "There is a universe you need to see. You must understand why he needs to end."

Brisa's hand went unconsciously, protectively over her abdomen. "How can a mother say that about her son?" Brisa covered her shoulders with the flexible sheet of strange metallic fabric. Some of the chill left, but she was still freezing.

"How can I live with what I brought into the world and do nothing? Everything is corrupted and ugly. We must burn the weeds so that once the soil is refreshed the flowers will grow again."

"*Weeds*? Don't you mean *worlds*? Destruction can't be the solution."

"Sometimes it is the only solution." A tear glistened on Mai'Sen's cheek, betraying her heart even as she said the words.

Brisa wanted to save this tormented woman from more pain. But to do that she had to find a way to save a universe she didn't know or understand. "I am so sorry you've had so much heartache, but I refuse to believe that is the only way. You claim your son is a monster, but you're the one talking about murdering people as if they're disposable." She sighed and looked down at the flight suit she still held. "Where can I change?"

"Here."

Brisa gaped. "I'm not taking off my clothing in front of these men."

"The first lesson you will learn is humility.

You're so high and mighty with your ideals. I cannot save my son, but I can save you." She glanced at Brisa's still flat abdomen. "And your child. Your pride is not more important than billions of lives. You will put on this practical garment, and you will do it here."

Tears filled Brisa's eyes. "There's no need to be cruel. My humiliation saves no one." She shook the black garment in her fist.

"Lessons, child. Lessons that I pray serve you well. Your acceptance of a greater purpose saves everyone. You must stop insisting you know what's best and learn to trust those that have been in this fight longer and have sacrificed more."

This whole pattern of reasoning was a ridiculous rambling of pseudo religion in Brisa's opinion, but Mai'Sen crossed her arms over her chest, firm in her conviction.

Glaring at the men, Brisa let go of the breath she held. They gave no indication they'd look away. She didn't know if it was to please their mistress or their own deviance, but she untied the strap at the back of her neck. She refused to look away or shrink like a wilting flower. If she had to do this, she'd be strong. The males gave no indication of emotion as her skimpy top fell away revealing her breasts. She shimmed out of the rest of her dress and let it pool around her ankles. All she wore were the delicate silk undergarments. The sheer fabric hid nothing. The men continued to look as she pulled on the flight suit. She pushed the dark strands of hair out of her eyes as she glared at them.

When she was clothed Mai'Sen stepped forward without a word. Brisa managed to keep her trembling hidden until the others walked ahead of her. It was then that she stumbled, but recovered herself, raised her chin a notch, and forced away her discomfort. She had a universe -- and a husband -- to save.

* * *

"What do you mean?" Ka'Sen roared. "You believe my mother is alive?"

Reven took a step back, but to his credit he didn't flinch like the other guardsmen who'd come to the bridge to update their prince. "Yes. If I wasn't completely sure I wouldn't say a word. I'm sure. Ka -- My Lord, it is your mother."

"How?" His voice cracked. He cleared his throat. "Father produced DNA. How?" He sat down.

Reven turned to the others. "Leave. Now!"

Without another word, the well-trained guards turned and marched in formation from the room without looking back. None gave any sign of emotion. Those at the helm left as well. Then it was just the two of them. Ka'Sen collapsed in the captain's chair.

Sighing, Reven knelt next to Ka'Sen. "I remember. We might have only been boys, but I cried with you. She was -- she was like my mother, too. We were so young that the truth was easy for him to hide. I had the DNA analyzed. It seems you have another loss, my friend. You had a sister. The DNA was tampered with, but our science officer was able to detect the truth. The death was a sister, not your mother."

Pain radiated through Kai. His mother had left him and started a new family. He'd had a sister. He'd always wanted siblings. He tried to imagine what a sister would look like. "My father's child?"

"No. She only shared your mother's DNA. I can tell things about her if you want to know. She was blonde. Green eyes. There's not much more DNA can tell us except for things that she was predisposed to, had she lived. Her father was Ajarian." Rev paused, and squeezed Kai's shoulder. "My anger must only be a shadow of what you feel, but not knowing who is to blame is an open wound. I have not been able to determine if your father lied knowingly, or she tricked him."

There was a pause before Ka'Sen sighed. "We were children, hurt in a cruel way, but that was then. Today I am a man and I will reclaim my wife. My child."

Reven nodded. "Yes. And I will be there as your servant, but also as a brother. I will not let this be another blemish on your soul, dearest friend."

Ka'Sen patted Reven's shoulder. "You are a good man and a better friend. I have no one to trust without you. Tell me how you discovered my mother. I assume this has much to do with Brisa's kidnapping?"

"It does. It seems your mother worships the Void."

"You're joking!"

Rev shook his head. "I have a twisted sense of humor, but even I'm not that warped. I wouldn't joke about this. I'm sorry."

Ka'Sen grimaced. "Does it matter? Brisa is my only concern. Get my wife back."

Rev nodded. "You have my word." He stood, bowed sharply, and left without another word.

For a long moment Ka'Sen sat. A mist of sorrow settled over his soul. What would he do if his mother warped Brisa? She was the only pureness in his dark world.

Chapter Three

Reven hated Ka's father, but the only way he'd get to the bottom of this was confronting the heartless king. He paused before the rejuvenation room. The old man had been here the last three months. Ka would never approve of him confronting the king, which was why he didn't say anything. He needed to redeem himself. He was the head of security. He should have kept the princess safe. Ka'Sen's loss was on him. His soul brother deserved better than failure.

"Enter," the hoarse voice commanded through the comm.

"Your majesty." Rev bowed.

He could only see the old man's neck and head. The rest of the aging ruler was obscured by the murky water he sat in. "Ha. Interesting. What can I do for you, Reven?" Curiosity made the old man's forehead wrinkle. His hair, once as thick and black as his son's, thinned and stood in disarray, peppered with gray, but his dark eyes remained as sharp as the talons of a carrion bird. He gazed unflinchingly at Reven. Rev did his best to keep the sympathy out of his expression.

"Your Majesty, how are you feeling?"

Servants buzzed around the old man. A young, scantily clad woman wiped the sweat from the king's brow.

The old man's eyes narrowed. "I'm sure you could care less. Why are you here, young one?"

Ka'Vin hadn't called Rev *young one* in many years. All the power in the universe couldn't keep death at bay forever. Rev shrugged. "Let us speak in private."

The king waved his hand. Everyone else in the

room rushed away. When it was just the two of them the elderly man chuckled. "Very interesting. I've been bored here in my rejuvenation tank. Very bored. How is my beloved son? He wouldn't send you to me unless something dire has occurred." King Ka'Vin laughed hard enough to make the fluid around him slosh over the edge of the tank.

"Your Majesty." Reven bowed again. "Your son doesn't know I'm here."

"Fascinating. What does Ka'Sen's lap dog want from me?"

"The truth."

"Ah, a very expensive gift. Very expensive. What truth do you seek, and what are you willing to sacrifice for it?"

"Mai'Sen. And whatever you require."

The old man's expression grew ashen and the grin slipped from his lips. "So, you've discovered she lives? The payment I ask is an explanation. Why do you want to know?"

"Your son has taken a wife. His bride is now the prisoner of Mai'Sen."

This time, Ka'Vin laughed hard enough that that he coughed until the water sloshed toward Reven's boots. Rev picked up his feet and let the little wave pass. When Ka'Vin stopped coughing he shook his head. "That woman. Saucy as ever. I loved her, you know. I did. She escaped my hold and the bitch took another man to her bed and birthed a bastard. When I had them killed I thought she'd died. It was years before I learned she'd evaded me. When I told you boys she'd died, I believed it. I learned some years ago she joined a death cult."

"I don't need an explanation, just what you know. Your son's happiness depends on it."

"Then I should give you nothing. Why did he dishonor me and wed without my permission?"

"Magic." Rev paused and let the sacred word sink into the old man's thoughts. "He longs to give you the dynasty you've always lusted for. Do you want your wife to win?"

"That is a very good argument. Look for her on Argular."

"Argular? Isn't that a toxic dump?"

"Vile attracts the vile and her comrades are as rotted as the dead. You'll find my beloved on Argular. I've been keeping tabs on her."

"Why didn't you bring her back?"

"That's a very good question. If you find out let me know. Love is a mysterious emotion that defies good sense."

"Because you loved her?"

Ka'Vin chuckled. "What is love?"

"Honestly, Your Majesty, I have no interest in pursuing a woman's heart." He could never tell this man that his heart was claimed, but his passion would never be returned.

Ka'Vin raised a bushy gray brow. "Love is for the young. Find it. My queen has given me joy and pain in equal measure."

"I think I'll pass on romance. If I want to suffer I'll go down to the training level and take on a battalion."

The king laughed until he couldn't breathe, and a doctor came running in to place an oxygen mask over Ka'Vin's mouth and nose. The doctor pointed at the door. "Leave!"

Reven followed orders. He had what he needed.

* * *

Brisa gazed out over the bodies. So many dead. Her throat ached when she noticed a tiny hand clutching what appeared to be a rag doll. Blood stained the fabric, making it hard to recognize, but yarn hair and button eyes distinguished the toy. She'd had a similar doll, the doll that was now with little Hoda, or had been the last time she'd seen her half-sister. The fate of so many rested on Ka'Sen.

What if these were her orphans? What if these weren't just strangers' children, but family? It didn't matter who they were, they were significant to her. Her vision blurred from the gathering tears, and she struggled to contain the sob building in her throat.

Mai'Sen's satisfied expression twisted her stomach. How could someone want this kind of suffering? The woman honestly appeared… glad.

They stood next to each other by a large viewing window on the ship they'd boarded. It hovered over a vast wasteland filled with bodies. Automated cargo transports traveled a path back and forth. More bodies tumbled out as the newest arrival dumped its burden in the pit. No life stirred on this planet. The ecosystem had been destroyed in a war dating back to the founding.

Panic skipped through Brisa's heart, causing her pain, forcing her to look away from the carnage. "Why are you showing me this?"

"The victims of progress are laid to rest in the pit. Here, on this stinking toxic world, the dead are left to rot. Your *husband* condones this -- caused this. He may not have taken these lives, but they are on his shoulders. Are you sure you think he's redeemable?"

Pausing, Brisa searched her soul before deciding. "Yes. This conquest started before he was born. Someone has to end it. Why *not* your son?"

"You haven't met his father, have you?"

Shrugging, Brisa sighed. "We are not our parents. He's as much your child as he is his father's. Why do you refuse to have faith in him?"

Mai'Sen scoffed. "Faith? I have come to believe in a great many things; however, the intrinsic goodness of people is not one of them. I have faith that the world will burn."

Brisa held Mai'Sen's gaze. "I am sorry for you. Truly. The darkness you see blinds you to anything else. I hope you'll see the light again. Let me go back to him. Give me the chance to show you how wrong you are."

Mai'Sen shook her head, frowning. "Even after seeing all this you still want to return to him?"

"I… I know I can save him."

"A savior complex. I should have guessed. I admire your dream, but you're a fool. If you want to survive you need to see the truth. I can't risk you opening his eyes to his own power."

"If you've bound his magic, I can't help him. I barely understand what I can do." Brisa dreaded Ka'Sen discovering his own abilities, as well, because that meant he wouldn't need her anymore. "How do you have magic? Were you born on my home world?"

Mai'Sen shook her head, as if responding to a tiresome child. "There are pockets of magic on every world. You can't imagine you're the first person to ever leave? The royal family's obsession with power caused many born with magic to flee to prevent execution. You didn't really think no one was born with magic outside the noble houses?"

Brisa flushed. The fact she was born on the wrong side of the blanket and had magic had never made her consider that other noble families who had a trace of magic might have bastard children too. "I... I guess not. You're right, it can't possibly be as neat and tidy as that."

"My mother fled when she was pregnant with me." Mai'Sen grinned. "She was of the noble line, and my father was a commoner descended from a defunct noble house. I inherited magic from both my parents. I didn't flaunt my magic, but I also didn't hide it. That was my doom. Ka'Vin demanded me, and my terrified father didn't even protest." Sadness passed over her expression like a shadow. "I've noticed you haven't used your magic. Is that because you're afraid, or have you never tried? Keeping you in the cold was a test. You failed. But if I couldn't sense your magic, I'd have assumed Ka'Sen was mistaken about you."

Brisa scowled. She didn't know why this woman's criticism bothered her, but it did. "I've had to walk a very fine line my whole life. I've learned to get by without relying on magic."

"Now lives depend on you using your magic," Mai'Sen replied. Outside, the sounds of the heartless machines working made the words far more ominous. "Your own life and the life of your unborn depend on you having the courage to embrace what lives in you. Be your power."

Narrowing her eyes, Brisa glared at Mai'Sen for a long moment. When Mai'Sen didn't flinch under Brisa's ire, Brisa turned her attention back to the terrible view. Fixated by the desecration, she tried to imagine who these people had been. Dumping bodies in a wasteland was cheaper than incinerating them. Automation made it easier to hide the tragic field of death. Another load of bodies, she counted fifteen, fell. A blonde woman clutched something to her chest, Brisa leaned closer to the thick glass to get a better look. Squinting, she made out a strange curly piece of metal. This corpse maintained her grip on the artifact even in death. There was a hint of determination on her slack features. "What's she holding?"

"*Omni*, the symbol for God on a world far from here. I thought they were dressed like Terareans. They come from a very industrial world. These people work hard for very little. The worship of the *Omni* is the only thing of value they have, and that's the biggest crime in the galaxy."

"Crime?" Brisa tried to get a better look at the icon, but the bodies shifted farther into the pit and out of sight. This determined woman disappeared, lost to the world of the living completely. "Rest in peace," Brisa whispered. She looked for a long time at the place where the woman had been buried. She realized she felt tired, exhausted really, as the weight of grief grew heavier. When the hair on the back of her neck rose, she glanced sharply at Mai'Sen. The woman gazed at her with such intensity it gave Brisa the chills.

"There are crimes you can't even imagine happening everywhere on every world, but these people were created to work so others could enjoy labor-free lives."

"Created?"

Mai'Sen rubbed the furrows between her eyes. She looked aged. Maybe it was the weird greenish light filtering into the room from the dead planet, but Brisa thought she saw moisture in the corners of Mai'Sen's eyes. "The planet was terraformed, and lab-grown workers were placed on the planet. They were told if they worked hard they'd be loved and rewarded by their creator. Work, slavery, is the only thing they value. The entire culture was founded on pleasing the *Omni*. That great and powerful being wanted them to manufacture until they died of exhaustion. The average life span is forty-five. They will beat each other to death if they suspect anyone of laziness."

Brisa gaped out the window and tried to imagine the terrible place. She couldn't. It was just beyond anything in her experience.

Mai'Sen sighed. "They endure extreme poverty on a polluted planet. They eat a subsistence diet that often lacks proper minerals and vitamins. They breed. They work. They die, all for the glory of *Omni*. Some have tried to spread the truth, but the people are so deeply loyal to their beliefs, largely due to genetic engineering for the trait, they typically murder any people who try enlightening the population. To make this ugliness unforgivable, *Omni* is the name of the corporation that owns the planet. They created these people and for three hundred years they've worked the inhabitants to death for the sake of a sham religion. These people die so old men can live richly on a distant world free of pollution. The people who benefit from *Omni* have little care or thought about the horrors of Tera."

"Can't we show them this?"

"They see it. A small group of activists keep sights like this in protests and foremost in the political arena, but wealth and comfort trump kindness. When the darkness is depicted the powers-that-be are quick to pull out vids of the people proclaiming their joy to work. I've even heard they will take people off Tera who are sick or hurt to demonstrate how deeply the people love working. When given luxury and the chance to recuperate they usually find a way to end their life out of shame. Death by hard work is the way to *Omni's* heaven. They are working for the best afterlife, but when you see this it makes the lifetime of hell they suffer so much more terrible. Those people started working at seven years old. The parents let *Omni*-owned institutions raise and indoctrinate the children from birth. Most families only have contact one day a week, and that ends on the child's seventh birthday."

As Brisa looked out at the sorrow stretching beyond the horizon, she wept. Her shoulders shook as silent sobs gripped her. She thought of her littles. What if the orphans in her village were subjected to a life like this? As a foundling, she knew the loneliness of having no family. Anger burned through her. Yet, she had no idea where to direct the anger that was taking root as darkness in her heart. "How do we stop this?"

"*We* don't," Mai'Sen said. "You do."

Brisa wiped her sticky face with the back of her hand. "How?" There was a desperate quality in the way she wailed the word.

"Look at that crane. Really look. Focus how you feel right now on the joints and the track it's rolling on. Make it stop. I know it's not much, but if you can do that maybe you can stop those transports over there. Maybe -- possibly you can take down the whole operation. There are many more all over this planet. It's not much, but it's something. Magic. We stop them together. A little power here and there and others will have courage. Rebellion starts with one brave little flame that finds the dry leaves and burns the world to ash. Can you be that flame?"

"I don't want to turn everything to ash. I just want to stop the bad things."

"Everywhere there are people there are bad things. Some are just more clearly terrible than others. Your past is a good example of bad things that are normalized, but still terrible."

"What do you know of my life? We've just met."

"Our spies keep a very close watch on my son. They learned all they could. They knew he'd married the wrong sister before he did. I know more about you than you know about yourself."

Something angry raged through Brisa. "You can -- can rot with the dead -- horrid witch!" She'd always been careful with her words, but anger made her cruel.

Chuckling, Mai'Sen shook her head, grinning. "Is that the best you can do? You are as sweet and naïve as I'd been warned. Poor child." Real remorse changed her expression. "I am so sorry you found yourself caught up in this battle. I have a lot of work to do with you."

"Just let me go. Please." Tears blurred Brisa's vision as she croaked out the plea. She was so tired and beaten down by the sorrow.

"You're an empath, sweet girl. That is why this place is so hard on you. Your magic is some of the rarest and most powerful. You have the power to heal hearts, but also to burn worlds. I *need* you to learn to grow that flame. You must burn all this pain away."

"If I can heal hearts, why don't you believe I can save my husband? He's not a bad man. He didn't put me in this mess, Val'Trea did. Let me try to save him."

Something indefinable in Mai'Sen's narrowing eyes and tightening mouth made Brisa hope... and then the flare of emotion was gone. "I must do what is best for all. Do you really believe he is worth the lives of trillions?"

"To me, yes. He should be to you, as well. You might not have been able to be his mother when he was small, but it's not too late."

Mai'Sen stretched out her arm and invisible heat seared Brisa, knocking her off her feet. Disorientation and fear were all she knew for a moment, and then stars danced before her eyes as her head hit the wall.

Brisa's hands went instinctively to her still flat abdomen. Everything glowed. The room sparked with diamonds and the air seemed to vibrate.

"You will not use your power on me! I am more powerful than you will ever be, little girl! I should kill you. Convincing you of the truth might not be worth the work."

Brisa's eyes opened wide and she gaped at Mai'Sen as she realized she'd created the wave of force. Every muscle ached as she lay recovering. Magic vibrated around her, making the hair on the back of her neck stand up. She didn't know what had happened, but terror for her child had stirred something inside her. *Is my baby okay? How do I save -- everyone?* She didn't want to hurt Mai'Sen. Honestly, she had no idea how to counterattack, but she needed to protect herself. Wiggling and pushing herself to her knees she stood on wobbling legs. Her chin raised a notch. "I am not ready to die."

"Courage and stupidity often look alike." Mai'Sen raised her arm. "It's often hard to tell them apart until one of them kills you."

Brisa imagined a blanket wrapping around herself from head to toe. Mai'Sen's brow furrowed. She stretched her arms out in front of her until they shook. Brisa clung tighter to her imaginary blanket, and then when the old woman's eyes grew bluer and her expression pinched Brisa threw off the blanket, deflecting, before wrapping herself in the unseen protection again. Mai'Sen stumbled and went to her knees. Brisa resisted her urge to go to the woman and help her. It was hard, but she stood her ground, ready. "I'm sorry."

Mai'Sen seemed to have trouble breathing. "You surprise me, child."

"I am no child."

The ship's viewing platform shook violently. Brisa hit the wall, but managed to stay upright. Mai'Sen lay flat on her stomach, sprawled on the grated floor.

Coughing, Brisa smelled the smoke before she saw the darkness creeping under the door. Several smaller crafts swooped across the death field toward the ship. Another explosion shook the floor under her feet. Forcing her fear aside, she went to Mai'Sen and knelt. "Are you okay?" She used a gentle touch as she rolled the older woman to her back. "We need to get away from here. We're under attack. Wake up, please."

Mai'Sen's eyes popped open and Brisa had no time to pull away as the older woman gripped her neck. Instinct made Brisa clutch the older woman's fingers as she tried to free herself from the chokehold. She didn't have to worry about the fire. Death was here. Determination burned in her murderous eyes. Hate burned there too. In blue eyes, so much like Ka'Sen's, Brisa saw her end. Everything grew blurry.

Chapter Four

Reven pushed the curly black flyaway strands of hair off Brisa's forehead. He'd let no one else touch her. She belonged to Ka'Sen and he'd see her returned. His side ached. He'd lost a lot of blood, but he didn't let his comrades see his injury. He watched the prisoner being removed, struggling. Mai'Sen had barely aged in twenty years. Perhaps it was magic, or maybe she wore revenge well, but the woman looked good for her reunion with her family.

Ka'Vin would surely make her pay for each of her years away.

Pity flickered in Reven's heart, but the memory of Ka'Sen's pain helped him quell the urge to protect the traitor.

Trelor, the head of ship security after his predecessor's execution, came on board. He pounded his chest once and nodded sharply in a gesture of respect for his superior officer.

"Is she secured?" Reven demanded.

"Yes, the queen -- traitor -- is under the tightest security possible. It is safe for the princess."

Reven pounded his chest and the security chief turned to leave. "Trelor?"

He turned back. "Yes, General?"

"If anything happens to our beloved princess you will die."

A flicker of panic was the only trace of emotion the man gave before he nodded and left.

* * *

The shuttle landed, hard, on the fleet's biggest war machine. Rev held his precious cargo tightly. He loved Ka'Sen in a way that he could never admit. None of the others tried to assist him as he stood. They knew returning her was his privilege and his alone.

Saving this innocent and returning her was the closest he could ever get to showing Ka how much he cared about him. What he wanted he would never have, but knowing Ka had that with Brisa soothed his ache. When he lay alone wishing for what would never be he contented himself with picturing the way Ka looked at his wife. What he felt for her was genuine. Her sweet disposition and courage made him glad that if Ka had to love another he'd found someone worthy.

She carried Ka's child. He'd die to protect the two lives cradled in his arms.

The ship's landing zone was unusually silent as he disembarked. The bodies of anyone Ka'Sen blamed for his wife's kidnapping were hung from the wings of Ka's personal warbird. Ka stood, flanked by his guards, as Reven disembarked last, holding Brisa. Ka completely ignored protocol, waving off his guard and rushing forward to take Brisa from Rev's arms.

The look of pure joy on his face hit Rev right in the heart. When Ka looked up and their eyes met, the gratitude in Ka's handsome face made the breath catch in Rev's throat.

"Thank you. I prayed to the gods, all of them. Thank you for answering my prayers. I don't know what I'd do without you, my friend."

Rev couldn't speak. He just nodded.

Trelor approached. Rev wanted to kill the man for disrupting the moment. "My prince," Trelor began. "The queen -- the traitor is secured."

Ka'Sen's eyes widened. "My -- my mother?"

"Yes. We must talk of this. I did not trust the comm. Brisa has had a full medical scan. She will recover. I allowed her sedation, so her recovery would be as easy as possible on her body and that of the child."

"Once more I owe you my thanks." Ka tucked his wife more securely against his chest. "Come."

The guards trailed behind them as they went to Ka'Sen's private cabins. Seven guards lined up along the wall across from the door as Ka and Rev went inside. Ka laid Brisa down on their bed. He sat next to his wife. "Tell me of the medical scan."

"I apologize for not sending it, but until I have found the spy I trust no communication." Rev waited for Ka to nod his acceptance. "Her neck is badly bruised, and she may have a difficult time speaking for a few days, but she will recover. The child is healthy as well. Your mother had choked her unconscious when I entered the room. That is why your mother was shot. She will also recover. I fear allowing her to live, but that must be your decision. With her power she could escape, but I believe she's here because she wants to be here. Nothing good will come of it."

Ka glared at the angry marks on Brisa's neck. He swore softly before kissing her brow. "End her," he said with steely softness without looking at Rev. "I have no mother."

"And your father?"

"Tell him nothing. Do it yourself."

"For you, Ka." Rev's heart ached. Once Mai'Sen had been the kindest person in the universe. Ending her life would haunt him, but he would.

"Rev?"

He turned back to Ka'Sen. "Yes, my prince."

"I owe you my very soul. I will never be your prince again, only your brother."

Rev turned his back so Ka wouldn't see the tears

forming. He grunted, blinking the tears away so the others wouldn't see. Blood seeped from his wound, but he managed to hide his pain and use his dedication as a crutch. He would not let his body give in to the pain.

* * *

Mai'Sen flicked her wrist and the battalion of guards dropped like stones, fast asleep. Closing her eyes, she exhaled. She sensed her son first, with his wife. His anger and pain were so clear he might as well be screaming his location at her. Then she felt the jolt of recognition. Far away, in the bowels of the ship, Ka'Vin suffered. His body was failing.

How dare he die on his own! She deserved his life. He owed her a life for the precious ones he'd stolen from her. Her index finger swirled in the air and every lock between her cell opened for her.

This was too easy. The whole ship had once been her prison, and she knew it well.

Blocking her son's agony from her vision, she decided to allow him to live, at least for now, as she focused on making her single-minded way to her ultimate target. After she watched her husband die, she'd destroy the whole ship.

The thought of burning everyone aboard didn't give her the giddy sense of satisfaction she had experienced on her way to Ka'Vin, but it needed doing. For the first time since embracing her religion she felt sure she was doing the right thing.

Each crewmember she passed slept for her as easily as her guards had. She'd leave them to die in their sleep. It was the only small kindness she had to offer. So many souls. Sorrow filled her. She hadn't told Brisa, but she, too, was an empath. That was how she knew her husband was pure evil. Surely there was no redeeming his child.

Another corridor brought her to the chamber where her dying husband slept. Mai'Sen held her hand on the door. Felt him in there. Hate clouded her thoughts. The beast could not be allowed to gain strength. Even old and sick he had the power to hurt so many people and destroy so many worlds. Nature called out for blood. The soul of her lover and child would not rest until Ka'Vin died.

Like the other locks, this one was no barrier. No guards protected the sickly, living corpse. Monitors showed proof of life, but the pasty skin and sunken features told her he was not long for this world. She had no more time to waste if she wanted to end him before nature did the job.

Mai'Sen put her hand on his forehead. His watery green eyes opened, widened, and he gazed up at her in fear. She smelled urine. Agony flashed across his expression and his yellowing teeth gritted as she pushed all her suffering into him. She made him feel what he'd done to her, from the first rape to this moment, she made him suffer.

A blast hit her. She shrieked, but used the physical pain to magnify her psychological attack. Life flickered out of the king's eyes. She'd done it.

Another well-aimed shot from the weapon brought her to her knees, but she maintained contact with her victim's cold flesh. "Is he dead?" She panted out the words.

"Yes."

Reven. Sweet, lonely Reven's voice comforted her. "Then I am ready. End me!"

Reven fired again. She sucked the energy into her soul and let go of it with her last blast.

Reven died instantly.

Mai'Sen held her arm out and watched the fire consume her with morbid fascination. The pain came in a momentary flare, but she didn't scream.

Death gave her peace.

* * *

Ka'Sen fell backward. Brisa collapsed, but remained on the bed. He'd never heard this code, not this one, not the one to abandon ship. This was his home. Confusion and fear mingled with his need to protect his wife. Scooping her up, he pressed the comm. "Bring me the children, my wards, and get my warbird ready for flight."

"Right away, my prince, consider it done."

The guards followed Ka. One of them sprang forward, trying to stab him in the back, but the other executed the attacker immediately. Ka didn't break his stride. Fire and smoke burned, but his guard made sure he passed safely to the ship. Brisa's orphans waited, looking terrified. They were well dressed and clean, but loneliness clung to them nonetheless.

"Brisa!" little Hoda shouted.

"Get them seated and buckled in," Ka'Sen ordered. He boarded first and got Brisa buckled up as two guards strapped the children in safely. "Stay with them," Ka'Sen ordered. He pressed his personal comm. "Rev! Come in, Rev?"

Static.

He turned to the guardsmen. "Get me a reading on General Reven's location.

"Right away, my prince." The guard finished buckling Hoda and hurried to the dash panel. He punched in a few codes. "Inconclusive."

"What do you mean?" Ka'Sen demanded.

"I can't find his life signs. He -- his last known

whereabouts was near your father's room. That's where the explosion originated from."

"And the queen? Where is she?"

The guard worked frantically. "Same. Also inconclusive, also last known whereabouts was your father's chamber."

Pain filled Ka. He'd sent Rev to his death. "Buckle up, it's going to be bumpy." There was no more reason to wait. Rev was gone, and Ka was king. He punched the code to begin the launch sequence. The thrusters engaged, and the ship performed perfectly, launching away from the ship with elegant speed. They sailed away from the ship just as two more explosions decimated the flight deck. There was no hope. Few would survive this. The most powerful ship in the fleet was space debris now.

Chapter Five

Brisa fought to wake. The soft whispers of children's voices sent her into a panic. She'd fallen asleep in the village again. Gasping, she sat up and rubbed her eyes.

"You're up!" Hoda said in a happy, singsong voice.

"I have to get to the kitchen," Brisa mumbled. "Cook will beat me."

"No one is beating my wife."

Ka'Sen's deep rumbling voice brought her back to the present. She wasn't home. She was on a ship. The last thing she remembered was his mother choking her. "Am I dead?" Her dry mouth and sore throat made her almost certain she was alive.

Ka'Sen chuckled. "Almost, but you're hard to kill. I chose my mate well."

She snorted derisively at him. Hoda threw her arms around Brisa's sore neck. "I missed you so much. I'm so glad you're okay. I thought you might sleep forever."

"I'm awake." Brisa held out her arms toward Boris. The ever-silent boy rushed into her arms and hugged her as fiercely as Hoda had. "I missed you both, too. Where are we? How did I get off that sad planet?"

"It's a long story. We'll be landing soon."

"Landing? Where?"

"My home. My ship was destroyed. Rev and my parents are dead. I am king and you are my queen. We will stay in the capital until after the baby is born."

She didn't know what to say. His knowledge made her feel cheated. "You -- you know?"

"Yes. The scanners told me. I will see that no further harm comes to you -- to either of you. It's too soon to know the gender of our child, but no matter what, I will love it. I swear I will be a good father."

His tone, the bitterness behind his words, made her sure he meant them. Neither of them had enjoyed loving families, but this baby would know only love. "I know you will. I love this baby. Ka, I love your child." She sensed he needed reassurance.

His shoulders relaxed as a small grin curved his mouth. "I know you do. You're too good not to. My offspring is lucky to have you as its mother."

Genuine and heartfelt, his praise warmed her. "Thank you, husband. What -- what happened to everyone?"

He glanced at where Hoda and Boris sat. "I will tell you when we land. You're safe now. All of you are safe. I've notified the surface to prepare. I've ensured we have a simple, but very secure place to live."

"What about my orphans?"

Ka'Sen grinned. "I have made them my wards. They are officially *our* orphans, and part of the royal household. I will never use them in an attempt to control you again. When you were taken I made a lot of promises to a lot of deities. I will be a better man. I might need some guidance, but I will be better."

"Am I dreaming?" Brisa was so sleepy. This all seemed far too good to be true.

"If you are, try not to wake, though I'm excited to show you the home that awaits us. I relocated the family to a very nice place outside the city. They did not mind."

Darkness covered the bright joy blotting out the bubbly happiness she'd felt a moment earlier. "You took a family out of their home?"

"Not at all. I offered one of my loyal subjects a better home and a nice profit to relocate. They were delighted to accommodate us."

"You aren't lying to me?"

He said nothing as they entered the atmosphere. Brisa glanced at the children. That voice inside her heart told her he was lying. Lights glittered over the city against the black of the night sky.

She was exhausted. For tonight she'd rest, and then she'd straighten out what had happened to the family when her mind was refreshed and her thoughts clear again. He wanted to be a good man, and she'd help him.

She'd save Ka'Sen before she gave birth. She had to.

The feeling of hands on her back caused her to gasp as she sat up.

"Shhh," Ka'Sen whispered. "I have you, wife."

She must have fallen asleep again. They were disembarking from the craft onto a rooftop. Two guards carried the children. Hoda was awake, but Boris slept.

A guard waited for them. He did the strange chest pounding salute and Ka'Sen nodded. The man held the door and they all entered. More guards waited on the staircase.

"Why do we need so many?" Brisa asked, pointing to the next landing where even more men waited.

"Because I will never lose you again."

"But you said your mother was dead. Aren't I safe now?"

"She did not act alone. It's too late to argue. I'm going to put you to bed, wife. Save your complaints for dawn."

"You're asking for trouble."

He smiled, a real smile. "Trouble me all you like. Just always be at my side."

His words touched her. She'd decided she loved him at some point during her captivity. She knew she would stay with him. Helping him be the best man he could be would be her life's work. She'd raise his babies and watch him bestow good things on the people of all the worlds. She'd be a queen of love and he'd be a king of justice. He didn't know it yet, but many battles awaited him. She grinned without mean to.

"Why are you smiling, wife?"

"Because I can walk. You can put me down."

"I like carrying you."

She mocked him with a loud sigh. "Yes, Your Highness."

"I expect to hear that from you, daily, in our bed."

She glanced at the nearest guard. "Shh, they can hear you."

"And when you heal, they'll hear *you*. Tonight, however, I want you resting."

Another soldier waited and opened the door to a spacious open concept and very modern apartment. She'd seen this kind of dwelling on the vids she'd watched on his ship, but never imagined living someplace so chic on an actual planet. This home was different from where she'd grown up in every way possible. They had machines to do the work of the servants, even the cooking.

When he set her down on her feet she noticed she was over the threshold of the doorway.

Ka'Sen must have noticed her looking. "A very old custom, but I will not take a chance with our happiness. I want to give you everything. That is why I picked a real home. Make this ours. Whatever you want, tell me. I will see you have it. Make the children happy and comfortable. I want the real thing with you. Today I choose to be a family. I lost the people who gave me life, but the only real loss I feel is Reven."

Tears filled her eyes and she felt his pain. "I'm so sorry. I mourn with you. He was a good man."

"Thank you. He saved you. Rev gave me my life back. I owed him so much."

"We will find a way to honor him." Her hand went to her abdomen. "If it's a boy can we name him Reven."

"Traditionally, the name of the child would be the part of your name and mine that indicate our royal lines, but we will start a new custom for our new empire. Speaking of which, this is the most secure apartment in the city. Look out the window. Do you like it?"

Brisa walked over to the wall-length window. When she looked down she saw the whole building rested on skinny pillars. Vertigo caused her to stumble backward. "How? What happens if it storms? Do you have ground shakers here?"

"The design is actually meant to make this safer in both storms and the rare earthquake. You are safer here than anywhere else in the galaxy. That is why I picked this home for our family."

As if cued, Hoda yawned loudly. "Brisa," Hoda whispered.

"Mmm," Brisa replied sleepily. It was late, and she needed to find out where to put the children to bed.

"I lost my doll. I can't sleep tonight."

"Get her a doll," Ka'Sen ordered.

"Right away," One of the guards pounded his chest and turned to leave, but then paused. "What kind of doll?"

"But I need *my* doll," Hoda insisted.

"Your doll is gone," Ka'Sen said, a little too sharply. Hoda's lower lip trembled. "But there are many other dolls," Ka'Sen amended. "What kind would help you sleep?"

Brisa tried not to chuckle at the impatience he tried to hide. Fatherhood was not going to come naturally for her husband.

Hoda rubbed her eyes. "Brisa gave me that doll. It was special."

Taking pity on all the helpless males in the room, Brisa knelt down and opened her arms. Hoda went to her and she hugged the little girl. "What if we go tomorrow and find you a new doll? Together? For tonight can I give you a special story."

"I really want my doll," Hoda whispered. A hint of tears stole into her tone and Brisa knew the girl would cry soon.

She looked up at Ka and the hapless volunteer. "Could you find her a rag doll? If you can't, get me some yellow yarn, and fabric. Something pale and another floral. I also need a needle and thread."

The man gave her one of the chest-pounding salutes before turning and nodding to Ka'Sen, who nodded back.

She looked at Hoda again. "That poor man has been through a lot tonight. He lost friends, and maybe family. If he finds you a doll, or at least doll-making supplies, it will be very special, agreed?"

Hoda nodded.

"Let's go to bed and sort this out in the morning. For tonight can you look after Boris for me?"

Hoda nodded again.

"You make me very proud." The child tried to hide her smile, but Brisa saw it before she looked up at her husband. "Where do they sleep?"

He turned to the guard holding Boris. "Show them to the bedroom."

Brisa followed the man. He lay the little boy down very carefully in one of the beds in the room. Hoda didn't go to the unoccupied bed, but instead crawled in next to Boris and stroked his hair.

"Now for that story." Brisa knelt next to the bed. She knew Ka'Sen listened from the door. "Once there were many lands. Some of the people suffered so that others would live happy lives."

"This story sounds sad," Hoda whispered.

"Give me a chance," Brisa pleaded.

Hoda nodded.

"As I was saying some people weren't happy and some were. Then one day a prince fell from the sky. He saw that not all the people were happy and that made him sad. He looked all over the land for someone to help him make the sadness go away. One morning he found some rags. He didn't know he had magic until the moment he wished for the rags to become a princess. He wanted it so much that they became a real girl. He told her what he wanted to accomplish, and she thought he was very good. This made her agree to go with him. In every town she would open her ragbag, and inside would be enough dolls for each child in the town. The grownups thought this was very silly. But the children were happy and that made the parents feel better. The prince learned that a little bit of kindness meant a great deal more than he'd believed it could. They spent every day traveling and gifting dolls to children until every child had a special doll. When the last doll was given out the princess grew up into a woman and the prince married her."

Hoda's eyes fluttered closed. "That's a nice story. I hope my doll will be a princess," she mumbled as sleep claimed her.

Brisa stood up. The room was large, but very plain. There were no toys. She'd fix that tomorrow, but for tonight she covered the children with a warm blanket. She wanted to tell the man outside the door to rest, but she knew that wasn't her place.

Ka'Sen took her hand and she let him lead her down the hall. It was dark, but the lights came on as they entered their room, adjusting to a dim perfection. A large bed took up the middle of the room. White scarves dangled from the posts and plush white bedding gave the inviting bed an ethereal appearance. Ka'Sen opened a closet and inside were dozens of dresses, along with nightwear, shoes, and jewelry. Everything looked like it had been made to fit her.

As much as she wanted to look over her new wardrobe, exhaustion made her movements heavy and sluggish. Ka'Sen helped her unzip the flight suit and step out of it. She allowed him to take her into the bathing room. The necessary and a sink sat in a small room. When he opened another door, a huge shower, big enough for more than two people, waited. Plush white towels sat piled on a bench. A long vanity counter ran along the mirrored wall. The ceiling overhead projected morning light over them. The illusion was breathtaking. It was as if she stood outside on a summer morning.

Ka' Sen shut the door, but she knew there were guards close by. He stripped, and seeing him naked made her forget how tired she was. She stopped worrying about their security.

"I've missed you so much." Ka said. "I want you to rest, but I need this. I need you, woman. I consulted a doctor, not just the scanner, and he said there is no danger to the baby if I make love to you. Consent. Give yourself to me."

His desperate plea broke her heart. She couldn't say no to him, not after he'd lost so much. She nodded. He pulled her into his arms and kissed her deeply. The reunion of their lips brought their souls together. She could feel him in a way that defied explanation. In a way, she could see truest thoughts. He turned her to look in the mirror. The lighting from the hologram shadowed part of her face.

"Do you see what I see?"

She squinted, confused. "What do you see?"

"The most beautiful woman in all the worlds." He picked up a brush from the counter and began to comb out her tangled hair, pausing to place a kiss behind her ear. "You are special to me in every way." And she knew he meant it completely.

Ka' Sen bent over her shoulder. Brisa studied his profile and watched the downward curve of his lashes as he closed his eyes, gritting his teeth. He kissed her neck again.

A man had no right to be as beautiful as he was. "I want to take you this second. Hard. Fast." He spat out the words as if they were distasteful. She felt his erection press painfully against her bare ass cheek as he leaned against her. "But I will restrain myself. I refuse to injure you or the -- our -- child."

At Brisa's whimper, his eyes fluttered open, and their gazes meet in the mirror. She wanted him so much her pussy ached and contracted as if her body was searching for him to fill her. She needed them to join and be one in that infinite moment of release.

How could she explain to him that experiencing his love was the most meaningful thing in her universe? She needed him, too, but ladies weren't supposed to want their husbands in the savage way she needed him. His noble resistance only made her want him more. She wanted to tell him these things, but her tongue tied with emotion so all she did was gaze back at his reflection and pray he could see in her eyes how much she loved him.

"You will -- must always stay this beautiful." He kept combing her long hair. Slowly he ran the ornate brush from the crown of her head all the way to the ends hanging at the base of her back. The sensation made her shiver. The sight of his arousal as he touched her made her hot. His gentle strokes relaxed her and chased away some of the unsettled feeling that lingered.

Brisa's eyes narrowed. "Why do I have to be pretty? From what I've seen of your universe there isn't a lot of beauty in it."

His expression softened into a sad, dreamy smile. "There is, if you know where to look. In all the worlds, you're the most glorious thing I've ever seen."

Brisa crossed her arms over her chest, fighting her urge to be wooed by his words because she wanted to explain to him that he needed to fix the terrible things happening like *Omni*.

He kissed her between her shoulder blades and rubbed his hands across her back. A bolt of heat arced through her, driving her to the edge of sanity, the feeling of his pleasure and satisfaction skittering along the bond and mixing so freely with her own, pushing them both higher. She'd do anything to please him and the realization terrified her. "I... I need you. Please…"

Groaning, he shuddered and pressed her harder against the counter. The pressure against her ass from his hip lifted her toes from the ground. He brushed a kiss against the back of her neck. She shivered. He sucked the skin, releasing it with a savage pop. Ka'Sen ignored her squeak of surprise. "How are you doing this to me, witch? What magic have you used to make me need you like this? I could satisfy my lust on any woman on any world, and yet you are the only one I want."

"You've magicked me, Ka. Your darkness threatens to consume my light, and yet I crave everything about you." Her throat tightened.

"Perfection," Ka'Sen whispered. His gaze locked with hers as he peered intently at her reflection and ran his palm down her back and across her side. The light touch caused her to shiver as his big hand came to rest on her abdomen, gently pressing her to him. Warm and alive, the caress made her feel whole in a way nothing else ever had. "This child is mine and I protect what is mine. You both belong to me, Brisa. Today and always."

Her ass rested on the smooth skin at his hip where the counter hid his erection from her view. His strength was all encompassing. For the first time in her life she felt wanted and safe. The way he looked at her, as if she was precious, brought warmth to her cheeks and made her breath catch. The connection let her know he meant everything he'd said. He loved her. His free hand ran over her bum, up her hip, and cupped her breast. When his thumb tweaked the sensitive peak, she gasped. He brought his index finger and thumb together, pinching and rolling until he wrung a cry from her. She watched him touching her, and there was something intensely erotic about him caressing her before their image. A voyeuristic distance gave the act a touch of wickedness that intensified her pleasure.

"I belong to no one," she lied.

Ka'Sen's grinned and there was a hint of danger in his expression. He pinched her nipple harder and she gasped. "You are mine. I can smell your desire. Shall I walk away?"

"N-no," she stuttered too quickly. "I-I don't want to be owned."

Ka'Sen chuckled without humor. "Yes. You do."

He twisted her around, and now she gazed up into his eyes, not his reflection. Her lip trembled as he claimed her mouth, branding her soul in the process. She whimpered with need and put her arms around his waist as she clung to him. It was too late to resist. She was his.

Always the predator, he must have sensed when her resistance faltered because he pulled back, holding her face tenderly between his hands. He appeared to be searching for something in her expression and his own became a mask of concern.

"What is it?" Brisa's voice was only a whisper.

"Who do you belong to -- with?"

She saw a flicker of fear before he grew stoic again. In that moment, she realized she wasn't the one who was owned. "You." So much power in such efficiency of words, Brisa claimed him.

As if a dam broke, Ka'Sen pulled her into his arms, holding her close. "Mine. Mine," he mumbled into her hair. Dramatically, he twisted her around to face the mirror. He pressed her down, causing her to lean slightly. His hand found its way between her nether lips to caress her clit. The sensation made her legs go weak, but her husband didn't let her fall.

Her wet heat clenched -- empty -- wanting. He

kissed the side of her neck, hard, then nipped. She gasped. Her need burned hotter.

From behind, he entered her, his cock stretching her. His hand continued to torment her clit, but he pressed his hand against her pubic mound, which made him feel bigger. She groaned as he slowly pushed in until his flesh and hers were joined fully. Her pussy contracted around him and they breathed hard, unevenly. The smell of sex filled the small space, and she resisted the urge to close her eyes because watching him in the mirror was the most magnificent sight she'd ever beheld. His dark hair roguishly fell across his forehead as his darker eyes glistened with emotion. He was studying her even as he mastered her body. Her husband. Hers. He awed her.

His pace quickened, each stroke hitting a pleasure point inside her. The angle was amazing. Her eyes watered as the first wave of orgasm hit her. She was awash in the joy of their joining and her throat tightened with the magnitude of her emotions. She loved him.

Brisa wailed her gratification, uncaring of the guards outside the door. Let them hear. Let them all hear. "I love you!" She gulped in a deep breath. Let him hear. "I love you, Ka!" Her arms shook.

"So tight," Ka'Sen whispered. "My love -- so wet -- so tight. So perfect." His hot breath fanned against her ear. "Mine!"

The wildness in his expression sent a little rush of fear through her. Hips thrusting faster, he wedged himself tighter into the small space. Pressing his hands against the mirror, he drove into her with a rough passion that made her wail. Still, she did not close her eyes against the onslaught of passion. They made eye contact as he spent himself within her.

A wonderful moment passed with her pussy contracting around his cock before he slipped out of her, half erect, with a satisfied sigh. Brisa shook. Ka'Sen pulled her hair back from her neck and kissed the spot over her pulse with a hard albeit loving firmness. Warm seed trickled down her thighs as he jerked her around. Once more desperation stole into his expression just before he pressed her to him for a long kiss.

When he pulled back she saw fear flicker in the depth of his eyes. "I cannot lose you again."

"I'm not going anywhere." But her stirring power told her she'd need to fight for love if she wanted those words to be the truth.

Command His Soul (Commanded 4)

Ashlynn Monroe

Brisa suspects her husband is hiding the darker aspects of their kingdoms from her. Each day her belly swells with their child, but her love-engorged heart has begun to shrink as she learns the terrible truth about her husband's thirst for power. Saving him by ending the injustice consumes her. She knows she can unlock Ka'Sen's magic, but she fears the truth may destroy him.

Brisa doesn't want to command worlds, but she does want to command her husband's heart. She's willing to give him everything, body and soul, but is she enough when she's asking him to give up the universe? Or does loving him mean accepting his darkness?

Chapter One

Brisa giggled as her husband's morning stubble tickled against her distended abdomen. Her hormones were in overdrive. She'd woken him by kissing his cock. Now he was being playful, but his erection bobbed between his legs in all its beautiful glory.

Days were the only thing standing between them and the arrival of their first child. Brisa rubbed the spot where the life stirred within her. "Stop tickling me, Ka'Sen. Our little Kutura doesn't seem to like it."

"Bri'Sen."

"Kutura."

Ka'Sen chuckled and kissed Brisa's belly again. "Bri'Sen," he whispered. "I will not let your mother give you such an undignified name." He glanced up at Brisa and winked before returning his attention to his unborn daughter. "It would be lovely for a common child, but you will grow up to rule worlds."

"What if she doesn't want to rule worlds?" Brisa tried to relax her brow, but she could feel her frown etched deep. "Can't we just wish happiness on her instead of power?"

Something dark passed across Ka'Sen's face. "To ensure her happiness I will safeguard her power. Everything she has can be gone in the blink of an eye. Everything. Supremacy is her only protection when we're gone."

Brisa placed her palm against his prickly cheek. Her heart ached. She still had a lot of work to do if she was ever going to get through to him. Ka'Sen turned into her touch and placed a kiss on her skin. His lips were warm. With her hormones so erratic, all she wanted to do was make love to him. Day and night, his naked body was the only thing on her mind. And as if he could read her mind --

Ka'Sen moved with the graceful speed of a warrior as he pinned her to the soft mattress beneath them. With the bond of magic between them she could feel his lust humming through his body. That need fueled her own. Brisa bit her lip and let go of the breath she was holding to slow her pounding heart. "I need you, husband." His slow grin made her heart flutter with joy, yet fear nibbled in the back of her brain. "Promise me everything is all right."

His eyes narrowed, and he pulled back a bit. Brisa let him scrutinize her, and through the bond between them she silently begged him to understand her fear. Maybe it was the baby or just the whispers she'd heard of war, but this felt like the last time.

She didn't flinch when he took her face in his hands, forcing her to maintain eye contact. His gaze seemed to be searching, and she sensed him trying to sort out her fears. "Why are you afraid? I would die to keep you and the baby safe. You know that, sweet witch."

Brisa nodded. "Of course. I don't doubt your love, but I -- I wish I could explain."

When his expression gentled, a moment of shame filled her. He had so much weight on his shoulders. He'd promised her he would make a fresh kind of democracy on all the worlds. Each world would get representation. Each species would be free to choose what kind of life they wanted. The whole universe waited for him to fix injustice, yet she lay in his bed begging him to fix nothing and everything at the same time. Brisa wanted to look away, but he wouldn't let her. His love poured into her through the invisible threads weaving her soul to his.

"I wonder if every wife has such high expectations of her husband," Brisa whispered, trying to defuse the tension she'd created.

Ka'Sen didn't laugh. He also didn't give her the relief of a new topic. "I would destroy and rebuild worlds if you ask me. I will never let anything harm our family. You are the only peace I've ever had. Don't you understand, woman? I will teach you everything." His voice was steady, but she felt his arms trembling as he held her face. "I will *give* you everything -- be your everything. I will lay universes at your feet. And you..." He leaned in and brushed his lips lightly to hers. "You are my magic. Your power will protect my empire, and our daughter will never lose the legacy *we* leave for her."

Fear grew instead of dying. Her heart thundered as a wild crescendo of feeling swelled and crashed around her. Hopeful. Conflicted. And terrified in the same moment. Tears filled her eyes. She blinked them away. "But..."

"No arguments." He pressed his lips to hers again, this time in a tender, slow kiss. When he pulled back his dark eyes glistened, making her love him even more. "It's just a fact of the truest truth. I offer you everything."

No other person had ever been so devoted to her. She realized she'd give him her whole soul, even the broken pieces. She was his and through the waves of power humming between them the certainty he was wholly hers gave her both comfort and worry. "What if --" She paused. *How do I tell him he has his own magic? How do I tell him he doesn't need me?*

"If?" He waited.

"Never mind." *I'm such a coward.* "Make love to me."

"No."

Her mouth dropped open.

"I will give you what you need. Domination. I must prove power and control can be a form of love. I love my people. They need to fear me. I wield my power and if I do it properly they will adore me, just as you, dearest wife, sweetest witch, do. With your time so near I will be cautious. Say our daughter's name and I will stop."

Real fear mingled with Brisa's arousal. He'd been her first lover, but she suspected he'd been holding a piece of himself back. Hiding a need she wasn't ready for. The bond of magic between them had hinted at his darker unspoken needs. He'd taught her to enjoy many things beyond the act of procreation, yet there was something more he wanted. *Am I ready?* Brisa nibbled her lip and just stared at her husband, begging him to understand her fear. His countenance gave nothing away.

Silence grew too intense. She had to look away. "I'm scared." Her raging heartbeat hurt, and her stomach fluttered.

"I know. We'll take this slow." Ka'Sen ran his hand through her hair. His touch was tender, at first, and then he crushed a handful of the raven strands between his fingers before yanking head her back into an arch. Brisa's eyes widened and she wiggled, her cheeks heated. She wasn't sure if it was from shame or excitement as he pressed his lips against hers in a punishing kiss. Her eyes fluttered closed.

A stinging slap against her full ass cheek made her cry out and her eyes opened widely again. She murmured against his kiss and tried to pull away, but he held her firm. Her distended abdomen was the only space between them. She noticed Ka'Sen was being mindful of that part of her body as he leaned over her. Some of her fear alleviated. His free hand cupped one of her now fuller breasts and when his thumb brushed the very sensitive nipple she pressed into his touch.

He chuckled against her lips and trailed his hand down her side to part her folds. The slick sound made her face burn hotter. He pulled back and looked at her. "What did I say?" The satisfaction in his eyes didn't soften the intensity of determination hardening his handsome face and changing him from her beloved into an unpredictable stranger. "Discipline can become a craving."

"I --" Her words broke off into a moan. He pulled her close again with the hand holding her hair and kissed her temple. Ka'Sen swiped his strong finger against her clit in a circle, using her wetness to lubricate his strokes. He knew just where to touch her. This part of him was no stranger. Her body knew his.

"Just let go." His raw, soft whisper grazed warmth against her skin. "You're fighting what you need. Let me rule you. Let me show you."

What if I give in? She wasn't sure she was ready to find out. Releasing the breath she'd unconsciously held she closed her eyes and just let herself feel. Each practiced caress of her clitoris was like a musician mastering his instrument. When she cried out, so close but not there yet, she became his music.

Her muscles clenched as his long finger pushed into her, stroking deep inside her. She wanted more. She wanted him. Her hips bucked against his hand.

"Shh, my love. All in good time." Ka'Sen seemed content to cuddle her against him, keeping her in a state of desperation. "Breathe with me."

She did. He inhaled and exhaled, she followed him, still whimpering as her pleasure bordered on pain. Then her breaths matched his. She shook, overcome by the emotion of him, and accepted his power over her. Her essence gathered around them to exist with his in tandem. The magic between them bloomed more alive than ever. His hold on her gentled and he stroke her scalp, massaging her. She was so close. But she let him keep her in this place between joy and pain.

His ascendancy brought her lulling serenity until his control was almost a drug.

Giving in almost feels like peace. Her orgasm begged for freedom. The need became a coiled spring -- tense enough she worried he'd break her spirit -- renewing the spark of fear. When she looked at him he gazed down on her.

His eyes darkened, predatory, but a smile tugged the corner of his mouth. "Trust me."

Releasing her hair, he skated his big hand down her torso, then hip, to cup and squeeze her ass. He propped himself up, looming over her. His other hand remained between her legs, swirling with confident movements, coaxing her body closer to the edge even as the pleasure officially turned into pain.

Her need was different now. He'd forced her to hover in the abyss between tension and release too long. This wasn't about him ruling the universe. His lesson was about the magic between them. Strained sorcery and excitement wrapped tight, while the alchemy of arousal hummed in the air, electric and tangible.

Brisa nodded, her throat aching. She couldn't manage more.

Ka'Sen leaned down. Brisa's breath caught as she prepared for his kiss. Instead he stopped as his lips brushed her ear. "I need to hear it."

The whisper made her shiver. Her eyelashes brushed against him, he was so close to her, yet a chasm stretched between them. Tears threaten. "I understand."

"Understand what?"

She wanted to scream or come -- but release from this terrible place between pleasure and pain required her confession. "Control can be needed -- loving." Brisa shuddered, her stomach muscles aching from holding back. She'd never been so hot. So ready. So wanting.

He looked down at her. There was a wicked gleam of triumph in his eyes. And in that moment, he was totally in control. "Come for me, sweet, wet, witch."

The deep bond seemed to swell with the magic and his lust flowed into her as hers seemed to pour into him. Being this loved, this wanted, this complete was good -- perfect -- even in the darkness.

"Come for me." Ka'Sen pumped his fingers into her faster.

And she let go.

"Ka'Sen!" His name was a prayer as he added another finger inside her and tilted the angle of his thrusts. His thumb rubbed her clit. Tears leaked from the corners of her eyes as the wave of emotion and pleasure washed through her. She wailed a primal sound that she didn't even recognize as human let alone her own.

Shuddering, sobbing now, she pressed against his hand. She was still throbbing around his fingers when he pulled out. "No, more!" Brisa half-sat up. "Wh-what?" Her slurred question earned her a slap on her ass.

"Shh," Ka'Sen whispered as he parted her legs. She blinked her eyes open and watched him kiss the curve of her right breast, the bulge of her stomach, the ridge of her hips, the curve of her legs, the inside of her thigh, before he licked her pussy. Her body jerked reflexively. He chuckled against her, and she arched her back when he darted his tongue along her sensitized nub.

* * *

Ka'Sen savored the taste and softness between his woman's legs. Her keening whimpers made him hard. Every sound stirred his heart as much as his cock. Contentment filled him as his wife orgasmed under his command. She was right where she belonged.

She was more than he deserved. And she was the perfect mate. Her light complemented his darkness. When he left her side, the radiance in his world burned away leaving a never-ending twilight. He was her first, and to ensure he'd be her last and only, he'd scorch worlds to ash. She had no idea how much he'd done to protect her, and she could never know.

Licking with broad strokes, he paid attention to how her body responded. Giving her pleasure was the most important piece of this lesson. She had to understand -- had to -- or all was lost. As his child grew inside her so did the bond between them. If he concentrated on that connection, there were moments when he almost thought he could feel magic inside himself. He needed his wife with him, but he needed to keep her safe. After she'd been taken he realized just how much she meant to him, and he never wanted to feel that kind of panic again.

Brisa's mewlish noises delighted him. She was amazing. He licked faster. She was his. She made him whole. Her knees clamped against his head. She jerked when his laugh rumbled against her pussy. Loving her with his mouth was his favorite thing to do with her, but his aching cock stirred. He'd have to be cautious or he'd spill his seed before he entered her. The sight of her on her back, filled with his babe, and totally his was erotic beyond words. She was the only person in the universe that mattered.

Ka'Sen worshiped at the altar of her femininity. Licking her, entirely focused on her needs, gave him a joy he couldn't fully explain. He'd never done this with past lovers. He'd never been willing to debase himself for another's pleasure. Oddly, her total submission to the act made him feel powerful.

The coarse hair brushing his nose smelled of her natural perfume. Ka'Sen rolled her clit against his tongue in circles. Her noises intensified, breathy and demanding. She needed no coaxing to be loud. His cock jerked. He needed her soon. Very soon.

Glancing up, he was stunned by her ethereal beauty. Brisa's pale cheeks flushed. Her fingers clutched the bed sheets. She writhed elegantly. Everything she did made him proud to call her his, even sex.

Ka'Sen had prolonged this to the end of his endurance. He might be a god in his people's eyes, but at this moment he was a humble man. A man with needs. A man surrounded by the scent of his wife's desire. He rose above her. She lay stretched across their bed, totally vulnerable, completely submissive, and very ready. The proof of their love rounded her belly, but that only made her more beautiful to him.

"You're the only person in the entire universe who matters." Ka'Sen pulled her toward him. He nudged her with his cock until he found her slick entrance. With a single thrust she accepted him -- all of him. Groaning, he stilled. "I'm so godsdamn close." He kissed her temple. "Sweet, sweet witch. I love you."

Brisa rocked against him, moaning. "Please!"

He could deny her nothing. Ka'Sen fucked her, hard. Her legs wrapped around his hips and he closed his eyes. Every inch of her warm heat welcomed him. "So tight," he murmured. He thrust harder, faster. The beautiful friction took him to a place beyond this world. Through the bond he felt her shatter as they both came.

Ka'Sen roll her over, clutching her to his chest as his beloved let out a drawn-out sob, shaking from the last of her orgasm. Her tears morphed into messy sobs as he stroked her hair. "I'm here." He kissed her temple. "Let it all out."

Her shoulders heaved. Ka'Sen stroked her back and the base of her neck. Her reaction confused him. Even through the bond he couldn't understand why she was so upset. He kissed her neck, smoothing the hair off her damp face. Then he felt her fear. "I would never hurt you. You're safe."

With each hitching sob she clung tighter to him until her emotional release trailed off into sniffles. Brisa whimpered, then sighed. "I just want to find peace, for all of us, for our daughter."

"I know." And he did, but she had no idea how impossible that wish was. "Sweet witch, I would give it to you if I could."

"And why can't you?"

His cock was still inside her, still partially erect. He held her tightly, kissing her face, wishing he could make her happy. "This is a complicated universe. Power is a dangerous thing. Giving it to the people is dangerous. Keeping it from the people is dangerous. Peace is dangerous. I am a man privileged to be in power, but with that comes responsibility. What you want in your heart threatens the balance of the universe."

"Doing the right thing isn't easy. Please, my love, do the right thing." She searched his expression and he was torn between laughing at her naivety and weeping because of that child-like glowing goodness. Her genuine empathy was beyond the scope of anything he'd ever felt for his people. She was too good for this world and he lived in constant fear goodness would destroy her.

He slipped his cock out of her and reluctantly moved because he refused to relax until she'd been cleaned up. Caring for her made him glad in a way he couldn't understand. Making sure she was safe, well, and content filled him with that peaceful resolve he felt when his kingdoms were in order. Maybe that was because her heart was the only thing he really wanted to rule.

Used to this part of the routine, she didn't protest as he gathered a soft wet cloth and a warm blanket. She didn't move, looking up at him with a contented and innocent expression. The relaxed look of her petite features stood as proof she deferred to his judgment, and her beguiling submissiveness gave him a little moment of happiness.

Each intimate, slow swipe of the cloth over her breasts, abdomen, and finally her pussy made him feel closer to her. She'd protested this early in the relationship, but soon learned to give in to him. He slowly washed away the traces of their desire between her legs. She slept naked, because he insisted on it. When he held her he wanted nothing between them. The skin-to-skin contact was the only thing that got him to sleep when the strain of the universe weighed on him in the night. He would stroke her silken body and listen to her breathing. The rhythm of her heartbeat lulled him from his worries. Millions feared him, and he needed her trust. She made him human.

Ka'Sen covered her with the blanket and crawled in next to her. "You should rest. It's still early. I won't leave until you're asleep."

"I'm not tired." She yawned.

He kissed the tip of her nose as he pulled her closer. They gazed into each other's eyes. Her blinks grew longer and longer until her eyes remained shut. She fit so perfectly against him. Her even breathing comforted him. With their bodies pressed tightly together, he felt their daughter kick. A fear like nothing else he'd ever experienced made letting go of his wife and getting up to start his day a challenge. He wanted to take her to the farthest corner of the universe and hide her away, but that was not her destiny, nor was it his. She would stand by his side as he ruled. Even if all he had left to rule was a pile of ashes.

Chapter Two

When Brisa woke up Ka'Sen wasn't in the room. She'd fallen back to sleep for another hour, but it was still early. Stumbling to their private toilet, a luxury on the military craft, she relieved herself. Kutura was pressing on her bladder harder each morning, it seemed, and she felt in her heart she wasn't going to make it to term. The medical team assured her she'd reached the point where her child would do well even if born early, but the worry wouldn't go away.

Ka'Sen refused her request for a birth on a planet. He'd been born in space and he wanted his daughter to be as well. He didn't want his daughter's claim to the universe overshadowed by her having a birth world.

Brisa felt stifled on the ship. Sometimes she thought she would die from the stale recycled air. She just wanted to feel the breeze on her face, or maybe see the ocean. Right now, she'd have settled for a creek or even a puddle. Something called her to land, a sense of warning. Her husband was a stubborn man, but her requests seemed to worry him.

After he'd snapped at her about him understanding how power worked better than she did, she stopped begging to leave the ship, and then she was too pregnant to even consider it. She was stuck in space now until Kutura was born. Fear overshadowed the joy she should have felt awaiting her child. She imagined holding her baby. She hadn't told Ka'Sen, but the baby had magic. She knew because Kutura communicated with her in a wordless jumble of emotion and sensation. That was also how she knew the baby liked the name she'd picked more than the one Ka'Sen insisted on using.

Brisa patted her middle. "Mama will protect you, little Kutura. I love you."

And she did love her unborn, so much so, her eyes welled every time the child's consciousness tugged at her own. Her daughter was alive and real. She couldn't wait to hold her and see her. Pulling on a dress -- flight suits were far too restrictive given her current size -- she found her shoes. She decided to surprise the orphans in her care with fresh morning cakes. She had access to the kitchens, given her position, and real food would be a treat. The standard nutrition-rich rations kept her full and alive, but there was nothing quite as nice as real food when her pregnancy cravings demanded a taste of her home world.

Hoda and Boris were very accustomed to life on the ship now. Ka'Sen always had a guard on them for protection, but they had the freedom to explore with supervision. After breakfast she'd take them down to look at the smaller fighters. Boris could name almost all of them. Even mute, the little boy had struck up a friendship with the head mechanic. The man had given him a model replica that could be disassembled and reassembled. The little boy spent hours each day taking it apart and put it back together.

Brisa left her room, using shift change to dodge her guard. She felt safe on the ship because her husband had eliminated the death cult trying to destroy their universe. Each day he showed her the progress he made making the universe better. With the many positive changes her husband had initiated since his father died the respect and love his people had for him had grown. She saw genuine joy when people thanked him. He was changing. He was changing their world for her. Nothing could feel safer or make her happier. She just wanted a moment to feel like herself and not the queen of the universe. When she decided to dodge the guards she also had to take an alternative route to the kitchen.

Weeping was the first indication something terrible had happened. Brisa heard both male and female sobs and followed the sorrow to the civilian sleeping quarters. Bunks were built into the walls three high. Each bunk had a row of drawers under the mattress and many little nooks for people to stow their minimal belongings. The room had a sterile feeling. There wasn't much space between the rows, but a single walkway to the far wall was where about twenty people were gathered.

A vid-cast screen projected on the blank surface of the metal wall and rolled terrible images of destruction in what appeared to be a large city. The broadcast switched to explosions in a community that still had natural features like trees and flowers. The sun shone, and everything looked beautiful for a second, then bombs, fire, and smoke turned the day into a hellscape of death.

A view of a woman about her age running with a young child in her arms and three by her side caught Brisa's attention. The children struggled to keep up. Exhaustion and determination were etched on the stranger's face. The recognition of death coming for her and a moment of resignation flickering in the brave lady's expression. Brisa's throat tightened. Flames unlike anything Brisa had ever seen raced down the road, devouring everything. The other people running behind the woman howled with agony as they were burned alive. The woman stopped and wrapped all the children in her arms, as if she could save them with her own body.

To her horror, Brisa realized the mother was smothering them. As the fire took them the mother was as silent as her offspring. The horror made Brisa's empty stomach lurch. She covered her mouth to keep her presence a secret. She needed to know what was happening. Somehow, she sensed they'd shield her from this truth. Ka'Sen had been lying to her. He'd convinced her everything on all the worlds was changing for the better. She strained to hear what was being reported.

"Today on Alesia Prime, the resistance stronghold, our great king has weeded out the last enemies to the union of worlds. This disease has been eradicated. Those who are protesting the killing of children forget the germ of ideals will grow with them. We cannot abide this enemy."

In the room angry, disbelieving scoffs echoed. A woman wiped her face across her arm, each movement jerky with anger. "How dare they!"

"Shh," a woman standing next to her said. "I've lost too many friends. Please don't say anything that might get you killed."

"Things were bad before, but this -- this is insane. Alesia Prime was peaceful! My sister lives... lived there. She wasn't a terrorist. She was just a woman who was trying to live her life. When will it be enough for the king, when will he be done killing?"

Brisa's heart ached. She needed to know the answer to that question, too. She fled before the people in the room noticed her lurking. The image of the woman and children burning stayed on repeat in her brain. She stopped at a trashcan to be sick. As empty as her stomach was it didn't take long, but left her muscles aching and her head hurting. Tears blurred her vision as she searched. She needed a data pad -- any data pad. Burning worlds was not the democracy he'd promised her.

* * *

Ka'Sen nodded to the general standing before the throne. "Let him live, but demote him. Is there anything else I should be aware of today?" Waking up to his wife's mouth on his cock and then making love to her had put him in a very amicable frame of mind, even though the invasion of the outer worlds wasn't going as well as he'd hoped.

General Ackler bowed. "Your Highness, others have sent urgent messages to Alesia Prime, but only one message from the planet was received. I fear we may have a traitor on board."

Ka'Sen's good mood evaporated. "Then they will die."

Brisa's bodyguard, Mikalis, came running into the room. The man's pale face brought Ka'Sen to his feet. "Where is my wife?"

"Gone." The man sucked in a breath. "I -- she left during shift change. She took a path that is not under surveillance."

"By the gods! How do we have *any* area on this ship without surveillance? She's too damn smart for her own good. Set an alarm. She's to be brought to me immediately. Make sure this Alesia Prime business isn't mentioned before her. She is, as always, to be protected from the work of ruling. And Mikalis, if she is harmed, in any way, you will die."

The guard gave a brisk nodded and left the room. Ka'Sen turned to the general. "Finding the spy is your top priority. If anything happens on this ship I will hold you accountable. Send the tech team to me.

They were supposed to lock down every data pad on the ship. Examples must be made and punishments given."

The general nodded vigorously. "Y -- yes your highness." He turned, stumbled, recovered, and managed to still have an air of dignity as he marched away.

Ka'Sen sighed. His good day was over. He hated everything about what he'd done and had yet to do. Someday his daughter and wife would understand. Someday...

* * *

Brisa stared at the screen, mute with horror. This world was a nightmare. The worst part was, she blamed herself. Thinking back to subtle comments her husband had made, and bits she'd overheard she felt sick she hadn't put it all together. But she hadn't. Her life had been ignorant bliss while her husband destroyed again and again. He was on a mission to eradicate threats to his rule, but in doing so he was holding every planet hostage to his needs.

As a follower of the goddess, she knew true peace required acceptance of the many as well as understanding of other's viewpoints. She'd never wanted the entire galaxy forced to believe in her religion. As much as she wanted to bring people to faith, she never wanted to see her goddess turned into a prison.

Her hand rested on her distended abdomen. How could she bring a child into a world like this? Her husband had lied to her about so much. She'd never be able to trust him again. Her finger swiped the device into sleep mode and she tucked it away into her dress pocket. She couldn't leave the ship, but she needed time to think.

The alarm sounded. Time up.

"The queen is required in the throne room. Assistance is requested by all crew."

Yep, time was definitely up. Brisa frowned. She didn't want to get her security detail in trouble, but she needed to know exactly what was happening without lies or sugar coating. She was the only pregnant person on the ship and the only one dressed in civilian clothing. There was no blending in.

The sign for the cargo hold gave her an idea. There was a storage area that no one ever went into. The best part was there were old chairs and mattresses in the back.

* * *

The five people standing before him were not soldiers. Two women and three men wore the pale green uniforms of technical support crew. None of these people had seen battle. None of these people had trained for war. They were young, too. He required every person on every world to dedicate three years between the ages of seventeen to twenty-five cycles to his army. This group was putting in their years before entering higher education. They'd all come out of secondary schooling with promising grades and hope. Executing them made him sad.

"As you know you are here because you failed your king and the federation. Those data pads were not supposed to be open. You have also let too much information stream in. Panic over the fate of family and friends on Alesia Prime has disrupted operations and caused a considerable amount of distress."

The technical lead, a man of twenty-two cycles, stepped forward. "This is my fault, sir. I allowed favors to crewmembers. I knew and didn't stop it from happening. I also should have required inspections of all data pads on a quarterly basis, but with the upcycling we were handing out new restricted devices. I had no idea so many people still had old data pads in their possession without the restrictions. Please do not punish my crew."

The shortest of the women, a blonde, blanched. "Emil, no!"

"Quiet," hissed the brave lead.

Silent tears ran down the woman's face and it was clear she and Emil were lovers. This made the execution harder, but even more important. Others on the ship would hear about it soon and those data pads would be returned as if they were on fire. Ka'Sen sighed. "General Ackerman, please demand the return of all data pad models that aren't under the current protocol. Anyone possessing one after 19:00 hours will be executed. Please put me on the open channel."

The general typed out a command, and Ka'Sen knew all the older data pads were flashing his orders. He also knew everyone on the ship could see him as he looked at the doomed technicians. "For failure to do your duty properly, I sentence you to death." Before they could move Ka'Sen raised his blaster, and starting with the man named Emil he killed them each with a single shot between the eyes. The last one he killed, the blonde, met his eyes and didn't flinch, just glared. She would have made a good soldier.

"General, you can end the feed." Ka'Sen waited until he was sure he wasn't being broadcasted to slump back into his throne. He felt, deep in his heart, that Brisa had seen what he'd had to do. He knew nothing would ever be the same between them again, and in a way, it was a relief. The constant lying had been hard on him. He was ready for the secrets to end. She was his queen. She loved him and carried his child. She'd need to learn the cost of the dynasty he was building for their daughter.

* * *

Brisa watched her husband kill. All this death, for what? She couldn't make sense of his irrational fear. Love had clouded her judgment, but now she forced her eyes open. She'd misjudged him. Her feelings blinded her to truth. He'd controlled the news she'd seen. Now she was free to explore what was being broadcast. Seeing him clearly was like a knife to her heart. He wasn't the hero of the story... he was the villain. She searched world after world's news feeds. Everything with subtitles said the same things... fear. These people were terrified of Ka'Sen. She needed to see him as others did. Her beloved Ka'Sen was a stranger.

The first pain came the moment she accepted the man she thought she knew didn't exist -- it was as if he'd died. Mourning and labor united until her soul hurt as much as the cramps in her midsection. Fear and misery united as she shuffled around the space gathering supplies. She was going to escape with her child and Ka'Sen would never have any idea what had happened to her.

Another contraction radiated through her, this time in her back. She forced her heart to stop racing. A medic to take away her pain and see her child into this world would be wonderful, but as long as her child wasn't harmed she'd play out her rebellion. She had a mission, to save this world, and save the man she loved. Getting through this labor alone was step one.

On her primitive home world, she'd seen more

than one kitchen girl give birth to a bastard. No matter if the child's father was a nobleman or field hand, the result was always the same. The mother labored with the help of other women and no man's hand to hold. She'd attended many of these births, watched her friends become mothers or die. She was strong, and she knew what to do.

"We can do this, little Kutura. I feel your spirit. Don't be afraid." Through the bond she knew her child wasn't sure what was happening. "You're being born, love, you're coming out to see me."

The child seemed to calm, and the connections strengthened. In that moment, Brisa knew her child was powerful and brave. She could do this for them. She'd take Kutura away and her father would never find them.

Mai'Sen was right. Her son was a monster.

Brisa turned off the data pad so it couldn't be tracked to the room. She hoped her labor would be quick enough that she could sneak out and onto one of the unmanned ship-to-land transports. These craft recycled CO_2 into oxygen and kept a stable temperature to preserve the goods inside. It was a risk, but she couldn't let her child become a pawn for a madman.

If there was a way she could get Hoda and Boris away she'd do it, but they were better off here for now. She prayed Ka'Sen would be kind to them. He'd developed a fondness for them that she prayed wasn't acting for her benefit.

When the pain intensified Brisa fought not to scream. She reminded herself she didn't want the first thing her child heard to be agony. She used her magic.

Finding the small shreds of joy left inside she held onto those weak strands tightly. Her skill couldn't take the pain, but she tolerated the worst of it. Her heart broke and her soul shattered as she lay on the old discarded mattress, pushing. Alone.

Chapter Three

Two Years Later

Brisa carried Kutura on her hip and walked through the market. "Look at those birds." She pointed, and her daughter smiled as she squinted up into the sun.

Like any other single mother in the small seaside village, she lived hand to mouth. Aquatica was a world of many colorful islands that belted the equator. She'd found herself on the most northern island, *Radia*, the local language's word for sun, which was ironic as most days were gray and misty. Today was bright and a touch of warmth promising summer had her in a light dress. Her honesty and hard work helped her climb to the position of head housekeeper for a very wealthy shipper in the city. Her small satchel jingled with her spare coin and she wanted to skip. Having a day off was rare.

Today, because it was her daughter's birthday, she'd use her scant extra money. She wanted to celebrate with a special meal and a new trinket for her girl. Saturday at the market was colorful. Vendors sold local wares as well as imports from far away. She'd ended up in this city and felt blessed because it was much like her home world. She'd fitted in quickly and had found a sort of peace. She prayed every day for the goddess to guide her and show her how to save Ka'Sen, but so far all she'd done was manage to build a quiet life. For the first time ever, she was making her own choices and that felt good.

"Good morning!" called Samik Seafarer (a ridiculously common last name for a world comprised of many little islands). A typical hometown fisherman, he'd become her favorite supplier of fresh fish when she shopped for the household.

"Hello, Sam. Oh, those look amazing."

"Thank you, sweets." Sam grinned, winking. She ignored his flirting. He was so good looking, but her heart still belonged to her husband. Also, if she was ever found she'd have condemned her lover to death by association. Samik deserved a lovely girl who he could adore as fearlessly as he fished. "These monsters put up a fight, but I am the master of the sea!"

"Aren't you too young to be telling fish stories? I thought you said that was for the old codgers at the tavern."

Sam chuckled. "I see you brought your little one. She's grown."

"She's two years old today!"

"Wasn't she only a few weeks old when we met?"

"She was. You were so kind to me, a stranger in a strange land."

Sam's grin widened. "Beautiful strangers are always welcome here."

Brisa sensed he liked her gratitude. Through her magic she felt his attraction. If she were anyone else, it would be easy to fall into the life of a fishwife. He'd be good to her daughter and give her more children. She'd have a home -- love -- a full belly. In another time and place she'd be happy with him. All of that screamed at her via her magic, but she ignored the siren call to follow the easy path. "Some strangers make good friends and not much more."

Sam frowned. "I've never asked you about Kutura's father. It's been two years. Would you do me the honor of coming for dinner tonight?"

Oh, how easy it would be to say yes, and put her

love for Ka'Sen in a box. "No, I'm sorry. If I were able to have dinner with any handsome man, you'd be my first choice, but I am still married."

His eyes widened. "Married? What kind of ass lets a wife and child slip through his fingers? What did he do to you? I wouldn't let anyone hurt you. Married or not I would be proud to call you mine."

Brisa's cheeks warmed. She looked away. Sam was so sweet. His tan, work-strong body would drive away her longings. When she lay in bed alone, rubbing away her lust, missing her husband, she sometimes wished she could be the kind of woman who would take a lover. Sam was virile. He'd be a good to her physically and emotionally, she sensed that, but he was not her Ka'Sen. None could take his place. "I can't tell you how much your words mean to me. Truly, if I did not still love my husband I could love you. You deserve to be loved first, not second."

When she looked up, Sam's sad expression tugged at her heart. "Any place in your heart would be enough for me. Brisa, there have been no others since I set my eyes on you. Let your past die. I don't need to know what happened, but if your husband hasn't been here for two years he's either a fool or dead."

"He's very much alive, but yes, he's a fool."

Sam grinned again. "Blunt. How does a woman like you escape a man?"

Dark memories of fear and claustrophobia shook her. "Very carefully." Brisa cleared her throat. She was on the verge of tears. "Let's speak of something better. Tell me your grand fish tale."

He shrugged, amicable as ever, before turning on his charm. Sam told a tale of massive waves, monsters emerging from the deep, and comrades lost. The soft sea breeze smelled of salt and fish. Brisa enjoyed the platonic companionship and let herself be happy for what she had. Sam talked away, and she smiled. A cloud drifted overhead, hiding the sun.

* * *

"Your Majesty, pardon the intrusion, but you requested immediate confirmation of Governor Seasearcher's response."

Ka'Sen looked up from his data pad. He'd been reading a notice of surrender and was pleased every demand he'd made was being met. "And?"

"The governor said no."

For a moment, Ka'Sen didn't understand. Every other world in the federation had rolled over. After Alesha Prime no leader was willing to risk every life on the planet, none except Seasearch, it seemed. "No?"

General Ackerman nodded. "I triple-checked the message myself. He will not surrender. He said he was voted in by the people and would not allow a military stooge to turn his world into another King's Rest."

"And what is wrong with King's Rest?"

"It seems not every world agrees that we should have one universal law and one universal code."

"Idiots. That code is for everyone's happiness." Ka'Sen tossed the data pad across the room and it shattered. "I have sacrificed *everything* for these fools. Do they not understand what I'm trying to do for them?"

The general's head bobbed until Ka'Sen worried it would fall off his shoulders. "They should. You are a wonderful king."

Ka'Sen narrowed his eyes at the man's wooden tone and hollow words. "I am."

Ackerman's head bobbed again. "You are. You are."

Ka'Sen sighed. He'd given his people everything. "I must think this through. Leave me."

Ackerman tripped over his own feet in his haste.

* * *

The little teashop's bright warmth called to Brisa. She loved the tiny sandwiches and cakes. Milsent Bigfish came out of the kitchen as the bell tinkled over Brisa's head. Her big smile was as warm as ever.

"Oh, my, you brought the birthday girl!" Milsent was good at remembering dates that others forgot. "I made her a special lunch."

"How did you know I'd come?" Brisa teased.

Milsent winked. "What Saturday don't you and the little one make it in? I will have the usual, and a special surprise, wrapped up to go so you can get back."

"I'm off for the whole day. May I sit?"

Milsent's smile was radiant. "Oh, yes, I'm so pleased. I'll have Mr. Bigfish run the show for a while and have a bite to eat with you. This is my treat today."

"Oh no, I couldn't --"

Milsent cut her off with a *shh* sound. "Of course you can, it's my gift to Kutura." The older woman went into the kitchen and came out with a three-tier platter of delicious food.

Kutura pointed. "Cake!"

Brisa laughed. "Yes, and it looks wonderful."

Milsent put the food down and her husband followed her with a steaming teapot. He set it down and checked on a table toward the back wall. Milsent poured tea into Brisa's cup. "So, what are you ladies doing to celebrate?"

"Well," Brisa began. "This, and then I thought I'd take Kutura to that toy vendor with all the little animals and let her pick out a gift."

"That's lovely. I remember when my firstborn was little I enjoyed outings like that too. They grow up so fast, and then you have a few more, and outings become a challenge. Enjoy this special day."

"I don't think I have to worry about more children anytime soon." Brisa's flush burned in her cheeks for a second time that day.

"A young lady like yourself needs to go out and find a man. I won't ask you about your past -- you're not my chattiest patron, and I respect that -- but take my advice, find love."

As if on cue Mr. Bigfish came out with some hot egg pie. Milsent grinned at her spouse before he returned to the kitchen. "And make sure he can cook!"

Brisa chuckled. "Tell Mr. Bigfish if he wasn't already taken I'd run away with him. His food is divine."

Milsent cut a slice of the egg pie and set it on Brisa's plate. Then she cut a smaller piece for Kutura. The older woman cut the food into tiny bites for the little girl. "That will be warm; blow, and blow away the hot."

Kutura's cheeks puffed out and she did more spitting than blowing on the piece she pinched between her fingers. The woman laughed and Kutura popped the egg pie in her mouth. "Good," she mumbled around the food.

"She's so sweet. She reminds me of you, dear," Milsent said.

"That's so kind of you." Brisa knew Kutura didn't look like her at all. She was the spitting image of her father. "She's a good girl." What would Ka'Sen say if he saw her? Would he see himself as clearly as Brisa could? Brisa pushed away her melancholy.

Business in the little shop picked up. People were in to buy loose tea or eat late lunches. Brisa people-watched as Milsent shared local gossip. She knew who was sleeping with which officials, who was pregnant, who wanted to be pregnant, and who wanted divorces. This was one of the reasons Brisa didn't talk much about herself. She knew her past was a mystery the elderly restaurateur longed to solve.

Mr. Bigfish came running out of the kitchen and displayed a hologram from his data pad. Everyone in the shop quieted.

"Governor Seasearcher has declared Aquatica a free world and has broken with the federation. Today in the capital there was celebration amid the protest." People stood in the streets shaking their fists and shouted "Alesha Prime" before the broadcast continued. "The governor has readied the water navy and sky navy. He has asked every patriot to join the fight."

The broadcast cut to the governor. "We will not burn! We will fight. Today we become our own world, self-sufficient from the other planets. We don't need a king who rules with fear. We want our own laws. I have been elected by the people and I will not roll over for the king to put a puppet government in place on our world." Loud cheering erupted as Mr. Bigfish turned off the news.

Brisa exchanged a worried glance with Milsent. "I must go. I suggest you buy whatever off-world staples you can before rationing begins."

Milsent nodded. "This was not the birthday your little one deserved."

"It's not the fate any of us deserve. Ka -- King Ka'Sen needs to be stopped."

"Yes, but we are just women on a little island on

a little world. Let's worry about what we can do --
prepare our families for the long voyage across the sea
of blood and war."

Brisa raised her teacup. "To the long voyage."

Milsent clinked hers to Brisa. "Yes, the long
voyage."

Brisa stood and gathered Kutura in her arms.
There was no going home for her. She had to travel to
the capital. This was the horror she'd prayed for. This
was Ka'Sen's last chance for salvation, or her death.
Time would tell, but as she looked at her daughter's
face she knew in her heart even if Ka'Sen could kill her,
he'd have a much harder time killing his daughter.

* * *

Ka'Sen gazed down at the blue planet. It was
dotted with green specks. So much water. This planet
was worth a fortune. Shipping water to desert worlds
had made him very rich. Having them leave the
federation was not an option. Was Brisa down there?
Every time he came to a world he wondered if it was
the one she'd fled to. He wondered if she was even
alive. How had she been gone two years already?

It was ironic that the governor would choose
today of all days to declare his independence. The man
had no idea how dark a day this was. The kingdom
thought his wife and child were ill. He claimed he
would not show his daughter's face for security
reasons. The truth was Brisa had vanished.

No ransom, which he'd have paid fully, had ever
been demanded. No trace of kidnappers had ever been
found. They'd found her blood, and the afterbirth, but
no Brisa and no baby. Which meant she'd left him by
choice and that was unforgivable. If he ever saw her
again, he'd be forced to kill her. The people would

believe she'd finally succumbed to her long illness.

He was lying to himself, and he knew it. He could never harm her. When he got her back he'd lock her away, chained to his bed, and she'd never leave him again.

And he would get her back. The universe was big, but he'd find her.

Something nibbled at his brain. He felt her. Ka'Sen touched the cold glass as if he could touch the planet. Somewhere, on one of those green specks, Brisa existed. "Am I being fanciful?" he muttered as he peered, hard, at the planet. "Has loneliness finally driven me crazy?"

Alone, there was no one to respond, but that magic he'd felt when his wife was with him and they'd been happy seemed to spark to life. She was out there. He just had to find her.

Ka'Sen's generals were lined up, waiting for him in the throne room when he returned. They had no idea how he struggled inside, because on the outside he was unmoved by the idea of innocent death. Inside, every one of those people could be his Brisa and the child. He dreamed of the baby, his daughter, often. In his dreams they were always by the sea. She sat in the sand building castles. Her dark hair curled at the temples, just as his did if it grew too long. His daughter was so serious as she constructed her sand world.

Brisa's chin was propped on her knees as she gazed out into the water. They didn't speak. He felt her sadness, but she never looked at him. He felt like a ghost. Then the girl would stop what she was doing, tilt her head to the side the same way he did when he was considering something important and she pointed.

"Da!" Brisa would startle and look around. He

would wake up alone and with the scent of ocean breezes in his nostrils. Last night, before the news, he'd had the dream again, only this time Brisa looked at him first. "Don't," she'd said. "Don't look for me anymore. Give me peace."

He'd awoken in a cold sweat. The idea of letting her go was out of the question.

He felt her on that planet. There was no rational way to explain his feelings, but he felt her. He knew she was there somewhere. His excitement matched his terror. She was in danger, but he would not back down. Not all.

Walking down the row of his most trusted and willing leaders he noticed Ackerman frowning. He paused before the man. "Do you have something to say, General?"

"Your Highness, this world is no match for us. War can be won here very easily."

"You would battle them on their own world, they'd have the advantage."

"We have the weapons --"

Ka'Sen stopped him. "And they have patriotism. This is their world, they believe they are right. They'd fight to the death and many of our own would die. We can end this very effectively as we ended things on Alesia Prime."

"Alesia Prime was a mistake."

The other generals gasped and the men on either side of Ackerman took subtle steps away from him.

Reven would have said the same thing if he'd been alive. A lump formed in Ka'Sen's throat. Brisa would never have escaped if his friend had survived. He knew Alesia Prime was a mistake, but he could never admit it. "Kings don't make mistakes, General, but they can make miscalculations. Let us try one more time for negotiations, and if they refuse they lose."

The general stopped shaking. "Yes, Your Majesty. One more chance."

"Dismissed." The generals started to leave. "Except for you, Ackerman." When it was just him and the general he Ka'Sen cleared his throat. "You will think me mad, but I feel there's a chance my wife is on the surface. This is to remain between us, but I want you to send drones with facial recognition software to look for Brisa. Tell no one."

"You have my word. My lips are sealed. If your wife is on the planet, we will find her."

When the general left, Ka'Sen pulled up a view of the planet. He stared at the green bits of island for a very long time.

Chapter Four

Brisa gazed up at the glow in the sky. Ka'Sen. His ship loomed over her new world and she fought the urge to run to the nearest data pad and reach out to him, to beg him to still love her, to forgive her. But she couldn't. The goddess had led her here. She had a mission, to save this world, and save the man she loved.

The mansion where the planet's governor lived was beautiful. Brisa had managed to gain an audience with him, and after comparing her face to the few vids that existed of her short time with Ka'Sen he'd agreed to meet with her.

"Sir, I know you have a lot to think about considering the demands you're facing. I couldn't save Alesia Prime, but I'm here for Aquatica. I've been on your world for some time, and I've come to know the kindness and generosity of your people. I've never thought of myself as a queen, but I do consider myself a public servant. I want this world, all the worlds to flourish. I want people to come to love my husband and I want his legacy to be a lasting peace."

"What you want doesn't seem to be what he wants. How exactly do you plan to save my people?"

"These are *our* people and I plan to save them by giving Ka'Sen a choice. A lasting peace that includes my return with our daughter, or he will kill us, as well."

"What you're proposing is very risky."

"War with the leader of the federation, a king of well-known cruelty, is riskier."

The governor ran his hand through his thinning hair. The lines of stress by his mouth and bags under his eyes showed how great this decision weighed on him. "Do you believe the king still loves you?"

"I do. And I still love him. In spite of all of it, I love him. Our daughter is something he wanted very badly. I do not believe he will kill her. As long as I'm on this planet it's the safest world in the federation."

The governor sighed. "Are you capable of accepting the burden of every life on this planet on your shoulders?"

"I already have. The moment I arrived here in hiding, I knew I held every life in my hands."

"Is this a game we can win?"

"This was never and will never be a game. With all due respect, this is everything."

The aging man nodded. "Yes, it is. You said you hid away as a house servant?"

"I did." Brisa grinned. "I wonder if I can still have my position back when they learn the queen of the federation was scrubbing the toilets for the last two years."

The governor shook his head. "Why didn't you come to me and seek political refuge? I'd have helped you."

"I couldn't risk endangering anyone. I knew deep in my heart a day like today would come and I needed to hide in plain sight for this to work. It also helped me learn more about the universe. I do want to be your queen, but not your jailer. I want peace, not dictatorship."

"Now we just have to convince your husband he'd like the same thing."

"He has terms to negotiate here with me. Would you do me the honor of hosting a meeting between us?"

"I'll have the very best food and

accommodations for you. Do you have a means to contact the king or shall I do it?"

"If you have a data pad, I have a way to reach him."

* * *

Brisa gazed up at the moon. Her eyes misted as the memory of earlier filled her with hope and trepidation. The governor had handed over a pad, his own, and she'd punched in a code over a secure channel. Blurry-eyed Ka'Sen's face appeared on her screen. He tilted his head. Their daughter did the same thing sometimes and her heart tugged as she gazed down at him. "Ka. I'm alive."

"I've known. I've always known. How could you leave me?"

Brisa's throat tightened. "It wasn't easy and I didn't want to, but I had to."

"By the gods! You did not!"

"Calm down or I'll disconnect."

That seemed to take some of the heat out of him and he quieted. "Why did you go?"

"Alesia Prime. How could you kill so many people? Children! You killed children! I saw a mother running. She smothered her children before the fires got them. Dear goddess, Ka, to have to kill your children to spare them pain is beyond horrific. You lied to me about the world you were building for us. I don't want to be the queen of ash."

"Damn it, you were never supposed to see any of that. I was getting the world in order for you and our d -- daughter. Where is the child?"

"Kutura is well and here, with me. I want you to meet her, Ka. She's so beautiful. It hurts me to look at her because she's your image. I love her so much sometimes I can't breathe. She's smart and too serious for her age. She's so much like you."

"How could you steal so much from me?"

"Because I love you too much to let you burn the universe. I protected my child."

His eyes narrowed. "By giving birth in a dirty closet? You risked both your lives, so you could run away?"

"I did. It was terrible. I would have loved to have called out for help, to have had you holding my hand when the pain came, but I knew I'd never have another chance to leave if I went for help."

He was quiet. Then he scowled. "What do you want?"

"I want a meeting, here on the planet. You and me, negotiating. And I want you to meet your daughter."

"When?"

"Tomorrow."

"Where?"

"The governor's home. No armies, no bloodshed, no ugliness, just you and me deciding on what kind of world our daughter will grow up to rule."

"Done." The screen went black.

Brisa almost collapsed, but Governor Seasearcher grabbed her arm.

"We have a lot of preparation." Her voice trembled.

And now she sat outside looking up at the moon, listening to the waves. She loved this place. She'd miss the open sky and sea when she was back on the ship. Her stomach knotted. She'd never be this free again. Ka'Sen would have her tagged like an animal and followed. She wouldn't be able to pee without a report going to him. The knowledge was daunting, but if her sacrifice could save lives, she was willing.

Standing up, she stretched before nodding to the governor's security team and going up the stairs. Her daughter slept in the middle of the massive bed. Brisa crawled in next to the child and stroked her hair. Dark hair that was identical to her father's. Sleep might not be an option, but at least she'd have one more night of just being a woman, who had a daughter, who lived by the sea.

Tomorrow she was the queen of the universe again.

* * *

His wife stood at the center of the welcoming party. How hadn't anyone here seen her for the queen she was? Her regal beauty would shine even in peasants' clothing. His gaze went to the child in her arms and the breath caught in his throat. His daughter looked exactly as she had in the dreams. She was beautiful, and she appeared healthy. A joy like nothing he'd ever felt bloomed inside him and he loved that child immediately. She looked at him, smiled, pointed. "Da!"

Brisa looked at the girl with as much surprise as Ka'Sen felt. His daughter had known him in those dreams. Maybe she'd sent them with her magic. He smiled back at the child. His magical child. A child that could find him far away in space and send him dreams. What a blessing. And there stood her beautiful, cruel mother. Every woman he ever loved left him, but never again.

The governor walked over to him, nervously, and extended his hand. Ka'Sen shook it. "Welcome, Your Majesty. Welcome."

"Thank you for protecting my wife."

"She's only been with us a few days. She's been living among her subjects."

When Ka'Sen stepped away from the man he looked into Brisa's eyes and he saw tears.

"It's so good to see you," she whispered. "I've missed you."

"And you only have yourself to blame for that." He didn't mean to sound angry -- bitter -- but he was. He still couldn't take his eyes off his daughter. *His. Daughter.* The words seemed alive as they swirled around in his brain. He'd created this miracle by loving his wife. Nothing could be more sacred. "May I hold her?"

Brisa physically recoiled and pulled the child closer. "Soon. Not near your ship."

He realized she was terrified he'd run off with the baby. The sick feeling of losing a child was a horrific tearing in one's soul. The moment he'd seen the afterbirth he'd realized she'd robbed him of his child's first breath. Resentment caused him to grit his teeth. He nodded once, unable to speak.

Ka'Sen and his security followed the governor, Brisa, and the terrestrial defense detail inside. Brisa seemed to own the room. She'd evolved. She had a confidence now, perhaps from being on her own. He prayed she hadn't taken a lover. It was the first thing he'd find out. If his wife was in love with another man he'd take the child and burn this world with her and her man on it. Hate for the faceless stranger made him clench his fists. The idea of some other bastard fucking his wife and raising his child made him see red.

When they arrived in the room, Brisa waived dismissively at the door. "These negotiations are for the king and me alone."

Ka'Sen's security shifted nervously, and both the

governor's people and his glared at each other. Brisa cleared her throat. "There is no need for a pissing match, gentlemen. Leave us." Remarkably, her voice carried enough authority that both his men and the terrestrial team left. The governor was the last to exit the room. Brisa set the child down near some toys. "I thought they'd never leave. All I want to do is kiss you and hold you, but first we have some things to settle."

"You've changed," he said.

"I've grown up. I'm not a mousy little girl anymore. I'm a woman. I'm a mother."

"You were never a little girl."

"Fair enough."

"I just wanted to protect you and make the world better for you."

"Sit down," Brisa ordered. And he sat as she remained standing. There was something reminiscent of ancient warrior goddesses and mating rituals in the way she stood at the head of the table, ready to whore herself for the good of the people.

His eyes narrowed. "I don't recognize you anymore."

"Now you know how I felt when I left."

Gods, she made him hard. She'd grown up. This new Brisa was exciting. He wondered how her body had changed. Her sexy curves were appealing, but so was her mature attitude. He wondered how it would feel to have her mount his cock and ride. She had an unfair advantage as the blood left his brain to occupy a more southern destination.

"When I landed here I didn't even know where *here* was. I lied to the exporter who opened my pod and told him I was fleeing an abusive general husband. He took pity on me and helped me get a job with his friend. I was recently promoted to head housekeeper.

My employer was kind to me and Kutura."

"Kutura. I searched data bases for the name; how did I not find her on the census?"

"Because her legal name is Kutuatina and I shortened it to Kutura. Our last name here is Hodoris. Which reminds me, how are Hoda and Boris? I trust you were kind to them no matter what I did."

"Of course. Those children helped me through the darkest of those first days. Both are well. They miss you. Boris still hasn't spoken, but Hoda asked about you a lot the first year. She's taken to her studies of late. I'm very proud of her progress. I plan to give her leadership on the world of her choice someday."

Brisa nodded. Her expression remained neutral and he couldn't tell if that was intentional or not. Her new confidence was as infuriating as it was sexy. He ruled the universe, and yet this woman had power over him. He'd give her anything if she'd just come back. Pushing the thought away he turned his attention to the child. Holding out his hands he whispered, "Da loves you."

Kutura looked up from the blocks she was smashing together, smiled, and stood up. She toddled over to him and he picked her up. Brisa went stiff. He could run from the room, board a ship, and blow up the world with her on it, but he wouldn't. His daughter blinked up at him. She had her mother's eyes, but the rest was him. "I never stopped thinking about you," he told the baby.

She put her little hands on his face and gave him a big wet kiss on the chin. His heart flip-flopped. "You know that, don't you? We've shared dreams."

Brisa's eyes widened.

He grinned. "She has magic, a lot of it."

"I know."

They were silent for a moment. The baby studied Ka'Sen's face, curious. She had that look from the dreams again. He kissed the top of her head. She smelled like hope.

"She's smart, too. Everyone in town loves her. She's got a charisma that people are really drawn to. Your child was born to rule, but she deserves more than ashes and hate. She could be loved. You could be loved."

"Love will not keep her enemies away." The baby wiggled, and he set her down. She returned to her toys.

"Neither will fear. But love will draw loyal followers to her. Love will protect her from enemies."

"You're a silly woman with no idea about the world."

"I've spent the last two years living in the world. I've seen the hurt your policies have left. I've felt the hunger of rationing. I've watched children leave for required military service and then watched the parents collapse in grief when the cremated remains are sent home. I have learned everything I could about being an average human on as many worlds as I could learn about. Your rules aren't working. You are making enemies where you could have friends. You. Make. Your. Realm. Dangerous. You've stolen your daughter's future."

Ka'Sen stood up, slamming his hands on the table. "I have given up everything! *Everything* for this kingdom. When I go to bed alone and you aren't there I feel how real my sacrifice is."

Her eyes widened a moment before that unfazed expression returned. "We all make sacrifices for what we believe in. The real question for today is how much you and I are willing to compromise our belief that we know what's best for the universe. I want democracy and you want control. Where is the middle?"

Ka'Sen snickered. "My bed."

"This isn't funny!"

"No. You're right it isn't, but I think that's how this plays out. There is no resolution until you are home, and home is where I say."

"I assumed as much. I will come home if no other worlds burn. If you swear there will never be another Alesia Prime."

"I will not tolerate disrespect and rebellion!"

"Then give them compromises that feel like freedom, but still retain your interests. Be a leader, not a dictator."

"It's easy to say those things when everything isn't on the line."

"Everything is always on the line when you're in love."

Ka'Sen snorted. "Love? You ran away and stole the only thing I've ever wanted. You. Left. Me."

"I saved your daughter." Her voice rose. "I want to save you. You -- fool!"

"I am a fool. I was so foolish to trust you."

She glared and he glared right back.

And then instead of Kutura sitting on his lap Brisa was there. She jumped up as if he were on fire. Kutura sat on the floor, laughing. She clapped her chubby palms together.

Brisa looked down and frowned. "That wasn't funny."

The child squealed with laugher.

"I disagree. She has my sense of humor, clearly."

Brisa sighed and just like that the tension diffused. "Finally, something we *can* agree on. She is very much like you. You've been on my mind every day."

He said nothing for a moment. "You cannot seduce me into submission."

Her lips pursed and then she laughed a hearty, real laugh. "I'm better than I thought if you call this argument a seduction."

His eyes narrowed. "Have you been seducing many men, wife?"

When her face fell, guilt twisted his heart. She shook her head. "No. I've been faithful."

Relief flooded him. "Good. I'd hate to start off this democracy you crave killing every male you've been in contact with."

Chapter Five

Hours of negotiation had stretched long into the night. Brisa rubbed her sore neck. She was tired, but it was a good tired. Ka'Sen had held firm on some points, but others he'd given in on. All in all, Brisa was very satisfied. She yawned.

Ka'Sen stepped next to her. "Don't fall asleep yet, woman. You need to seal our bargain. The word of others is nothing compared to your submission. It's time for your discipline," Ka'Sen whispered in her ear as he put his arm around her, pulling her close. He led her away from the group. The only thing she could hear was her racing heart pulsing in her ears. Fear mingled with her excitement. She was so wet just from his proximity, she hoped no one could smell her lust.

"Leave us," Ka'Sen's voice boomed in the small space. The diplomats filed out, most appeared relieved, but the governor glanced fearfully between Brisa and Ka. His expression screamed terror -- terror for her. She wanted to reassure the kind man, but didn't know how.

Ka'Sen glared. "Go!"

Brisa flinched as Ka'Sen wound her hair around his hand and yanked her head to the side. He kissed her neck with a violent passion, sucking until the skin burned and she was marked. Tomorrow they'd know, they'd all know. She bit her lip and arched back, wiggling.

The governor fled as if the building were on fire.

"You have a lot to make up for, wife. I will punish you, but only when I have you naked, under me. When I have you so needy you are begging me for more. Are we clear?"

She whimpered, and her face burned as he ran his hand down her back, rubbed her ass, and then slipped his long fingers between her legs to find her pussy cleft. The folds parted with a slick sound. Even angry and scared she wanted him. She'd wanted him since she'd stepped off the shuttle and back home. To be honest she'd wanted him every day since she'd last seen him.

"What did I say?" Smugness colored his words. "A bit of discipline will do wonders. I have a lot to punish you for, and when I'm done I expect to be thanked." He yanked her skirt down.

She flinched at the sound of her panties tearing. They fell to the floor, leaving her naked from the waist down. "Isn't --" Her words broke into a moan as he swiped through her wetness and found her clit. He rubbed it until her hips bounced of their own accord. She made primal little yips as he caressed her.

"It's been a long time since a man touched you, hasn't it?"

She just whimpered.

He tugged her hair again. "Hasn't it?"

"Ye -- yes. So long," she moaned.

"Feel," he urged in a disarming whisper. "You're holding back. Feel my touch. Want it."

Brisa wasn't ready to give in to him. She wasn't ready to concede to his victory in the war they'd fought on Aquatica. But he was the winner. Her moans made it clear. He. Was. Her. Master. She wanted to shout with joy or maybe anger, but she wasn't holding back as she moaned. Her muscles clenched on his long fingers as he gently pushed into her, stroking her G-spot. She wiggled. "More! Mmm, more!"

"Relax, love, all in good time. I've been waiting for years and so can you." He chuckled when she bucked against the hand fucking her. "You like that, don't you?"

"Ye -- yes. Mmm, those fingers. Harder! Oh, Ka, oh!"

He slapped her ass. "Soon, but first you have to want me as much as I've been waiting you.

"I've wanted you every night!"

"That's not good enough. I wanted you ever single second for two years. I have punishment yet to deliver."

She moaned.

His guest room was next to the meeting room. He left her discarded clothing on the floor and carried her across to the door, kicking it open with his typical drama. She turned her face into his shoulder so he wouldn't see her grin. He wouldn't appreciate her amusement.

Ka'Sen deposited her on the bed and lay next to her. He unbuttoned her blouse, pushing it open to admire her fuller breasts.

* * *

She loved him so much she ached. They were breathing in tandem. He stroked her hair, gentle and soft, but didn't let go. She was leashed by the strands but didn't care. She belonged to him and with him. She knew it. He knew it. Brisa closed her eyes and let the serenity of their bond lull her. Being in his arms was like a sedative injected into her veins. He made her high.

He sat up, pulling her across his lap and his hand came down across her ass. Brisa yelped. He spanked her hard and fell into a rhythm. She only struggled for a moment before she gave in. Submission. Submission felt good.

She kissed his stomach, since it was the only part of him her lips could reach. He kept her head high enough away from his lap that she couldn't suck his cock. She'd have given her soul to put his cock in her mouth. The magic he now wielded hummed between them. The power felt like a tightly coiled spring. Everything was so tense for a wild moment she thought he might break, or she might. Maybe they'd break together; two broken dolls lying side by side, united by damage and the need to be fixed.

He slapped her ass. She flinched. He continued to spank her, but the pain was minimal. Each tiny sting felt good, not bad, and she closed her eyes. He let go of her hair and she lay boneless and at his mercy. His repeated slaps pulled a moan out of her. She lay across his lap, putty under his control, never wanting him to stop, but afraid of how much she needed his command. His control.

Ka'Sen kissed the top of her head. "There is nowhere you could go where I wouldn't come for you," he vowed. "I will *always* find you."

"I will never give in if you're wrong. We make this world a better place together or you burn it down alone."

He remained quiet for a moment before clearing his throat. "You're not in a position," his bare hand skated along her ass before he smacked it again. "To make demands." He pushed the hair out of her face and looked into her eyes. The moment was sweet, until his hand slipped between her legs, swirling to coax her closer to the edge. Her stomach muscles clenched, and she jerked, trembling for him.

"You want this."

The moment of truth, far more so than when she first made the bargain. This was about her and what she wanted. The anger and the tension morphed into excitement. Need hummed in the air until it was electricity. His hard cock was proof he still wanted her too.

Heart in her throat, Brisa nodded, unable to manage more. His touches felt good. She moaned. Her legs twitched from how much she wanted to buck her hips.

Ka'Sen's lips were so close she felt his breath on her cheek. "I need to hear it."

"Yes, M-My King..." Brisa shuddered, stomach cramping as she tried holding perfectly still. Pleasing him was all she wanted now. "I will never leave you again. I..." She inhaled sharply. "Am..." Exhaled. "Yours."

His triumph seemed to soar across the magical bond tying them together. Brisa relaxed, flush with relief and lust, tender warmth filled her. That feeling wasn't coming from her. It was her husband's love pooling into her. She closed her eyes and sighed. She was home. And so desperately free as she succumbed.

She mumbled a protest when he pulled away, leaving her throbbing. But before she said anything, Ka'Sen turned her over onto her back. He pressed kisses to her breastbone, the slope below her ribs, the little bulge of her stomach left over from carrying his child, the crest of her hip, the inside of her thigh, and...

He parted her legs. Cool air teased her throbbing clit. She whimpered, her desire hovering near meltdown. He licked softly, feather-light contact of his tongue to her clit, barely a brush of air.

Brisa's primal cry echoed in the room. Turned on and still sensitive from his earlier attention she shook and sweat beaded on her brow. "I'm so close."

And then he lapped at her like a dying man

gasping for air, her pussy his sustenance as he devoured her. Shaking, she shattered against his hungry mouth. His fingers plunged to fuck her mercilessly. The sparks behind her eyelids transported her to a world where nothing but the smell of sex and Ka'Sen's touch existed. Time lost meaning. His fingers were replaced with his cock and his wild need matched hers in a crescendo of rage and want. His pain filled her, and she ached for the hurt between them.

A new feeling, his forgiveness, covered her like a blanket and she snuggled into his love even as her pussy clenched around his cock, milking his seed. Brisa sobbed as she came, horrified, but unable to help herself she let everything empty into the bond between them.

Ka'Sen rolled her over and pulled her to fit against him, spooning her close to his chest, and kissing her shoulder. "That's right," he whispered, "Let it go. Let it all out." He stroked her hair.

Her emotions flowed out in a torrential outburst, leaving her a trembling mess. Humiliation made her cry harder. She wanted to stop but couldn't.

Ka'Sen's fingers stroked her shoulders, the base of her neck, and the hair along her brow. He kissed her ear. "We've been through so much," he whispered. "I'm here now, you're not alone anymore. I should never have lied to you. I should have known you were strong enough to handle this universe."

The knot in her soul loosened with each tear, each hitch of her breath, and finally the storm inside ran out of steam. Her crying trailed into sniffles, ending with a single deep sigh.

Her sorrow unlocked his magic. Ka'Sen's back arched and he screamed as light erupted from him, shattering, surrounding them both in raw power.

Epilogue

Three Years Later...

Kutura laughed as she ran across the beach. Brisa had slathered her daughter's pale space-dweller skin in protection, but she still feared the results of this blissful day could end with a bad burn.

A year ago, they'd never have been able to set foot off the ship. This day trip would have killed them.

This had been a long time coming... three long years.

The sound of sea birds calling overhead and waves breaking against the cliffs were beautiful music. Brisa closed her eyes and let the sun warm her face.

Ka'Sen sat down on the large blanket next to Brisa. She opened her eyes and looked at him as he held out a fruity drink, non-alcoholic as she was pregnant with their second child, but still delicious.

Her husband -- her king -- appeared awkward as he tried to act like any other man spending a day of relaxation with his family. He'd earned this after the tribulations of the Four Years War and the resulting treaties and diplomacy.

Together they'd made a universe they could raise their children in.

A woman came toward them, timidly. Ka'Sen's guard immediately surrounded her.

"Let her pass," Ka ordered.

The woman fell to her knees, tears welled in her eyes. "My king. It is an honor to meet you and the Queen of Peace." She glanced at Brisa, who was still not used to the dramatic nickname given to her by the people. "When I saw you, *Great Sky Spirit* called to my heart and I was drawn to you."

Brisa reached out and gently took the weeping woman's hand.

The woman swallowed as if she had a lump in her throat, and turned her watery violet gaze on Brisa. "I -- I thought I would always be a slave. Now, I have freedom. My husband left his master to return home to me and the children. He owns land and although together we don't have much, we have each other. We are together. Without the laws against slavery I'd still be living a nightmare. You saved my family. You gave me my life. How can I ever thank you?"

Brisa wiped moisture out of her eyes. "Some of those who were benefiting from your pain don't have such warm feelings for us. Never forget that your king cares. That's all we can ask."

The woman nodded. "I would never forget what you've done for me. My children will never forget."

Brisa squeezed the woman's hand. "Then you've thanked us with all that we could ask for."

The woman smiled, but there was pain in her expression. Brisa squeezed her hand again before letting go. The woman stood and left.

For a long moment silence lingered between Ka'Sen and Brisa as they watched their daughter playing like any other child, not the heir to the universe.

"You were right," Ka'Sen said.

Brisa turned to meet his gaze. She frowned.

Ka'Sen smiled. "You were right about the universe. This is a world we can leave for her. A world that will love her."

Brisa's throat tightened. She couldn't respond.

"You made me a better man. You command my very soul, wife."

Brisa gazed over the ocean. "It's the only

kingdom I want. I love you, Ka."

He pulled her into his arms so fast a gasp slipped from her. When his lips pressed to hers she knew he spoke the truth. Her love *had* made him a better man.

Ashlynn Monroe

Ashlynn Monroe is a busy working mom. She loves her kids and family. Her greatest joy is creating stories to entertain others, and she hopes they bring a little more romance into the world. She's been writing since her teens for her own enjoyment but decided in her thirties to share her imagination with readers. Ashlynn enjoys biking, camping, reading, video games, and filling her home and life with love. If she's not working or chasing children, you can find her daydreaming up her next tale of romance.

Ashlynn at Changeling: changelingpress.com/ashlynn-monroe-a-166

Changeling Press E-Books

More Sci-Fi, Fantasy, Paranormal, and BDSM adventures available in e-book format for immediate download at ChangelingPress.com -- Werewolves, Vampires, Dragons, Shapeshifters and more -- Erotic Tales from the edge of your imagination.

What are E-Books?

E-books, or electronic books, are books designed to be read in digital format -- on your desktop or laptop computer, notebook, tablet, Smart Phone, or any electronic e-book reader.

Where can I get Changeling Press E-Books?

Changeling Press e-books are available at ChangelingPress.com, Amazon, Apple Books, Barnes & Noble, and Kobo/Walmart.

ChangelingPress.com